核心素養
108課綱

讀出英語

核心素養

九大技巧打造閱讀力 ①

作者 • Owain Mckimm　　譯者 • 劉嘉珮　　審訂 • Helen Yeh
協同作者 • Zachary Fillingham / Laura Phelps / Rob Webb / Richard Luhrs

MP3
寂天雲 APP

如何下載 MP3 音檔

❶ 寂天雲 APP 聆聽：掃描書上 QR Code 下載
「寂天雲－英日語學習隨身聽」APP。加入會員
後，用 APP 內建掃描器再次掃描書上 QR Code，
即可使用 APP 聆聽音檔。

❷ 官網下載音檔：請上「寂天閱讀網」
（www.icosmos.com.tw），註冊會員／登入後，
搜尋本書，進入本書頁面，點選「MP3 下載」
下載音檔，存於電腦等其他播放器聆聽使用。

Contents

Unit 1 Reading Skills 閱讀技巧

體裁 / 主題	議題	素養
paragraph 段落 / language & communication 語言與溝通	reading literacy 閱讀素養教育	semiotics 符號運用
dialogue 對話 / culture 文化	multiculturalism 多元文化教育	global understanding 國際理解
blog 部落格 / culture 文化	gender equality 性別平等教育	aesthetic literacy 美感素養
passage 短文 / health & body 健康與身體	disaster prevention 防災教育	global understanding 國際理解
column 專欄 / animals 動物	life 生命教育	interpersonal relationship 人際關係
card 卡片 / families, family relationships & kinship terms 家庭、家庭關係與親屬關係	morality 品德教育	expression 溝通表達
dialogue 對話 / social behavior 社會行為	security 安全教育	moral praxis 道德實踐
passage 短文 / education 教育	reading literacy 閱讀素養教育	logical thinking 系統思考
passage 短文 / gender equality 性別平等	gender equality 性別平等教育	expression 溝通表達
dialogue 對話 / teens 青少年生活	life 生命教育	interpersonal relationship 人際關係

Unit 2 Word Study 字彙學習

體裁 / 主題	議題	素養
broadcasting 廣播 / daily routines 日常生活	information 資訊教育	media literacy 媒體素養
invitation 邀請卡 / life 生活	technology 科技教育	information and technology literacy 科技資訊
speech 演說 / teens 青少年生活	morality 品德教育	interpersonal relationship 人際關係
passage 短文 / holidays & festivals 假日與節日	environment 環境教育	physical and mental wellness 身心素質
passage 短文 / arts & literature 藝術與文學	multiculturalism 多元文化教育	artistic appreciation 藝術涵養
dialogue 對話 / health & body 健康與身體	morality 品德教育	logical thinking 系統思考
advertisement 廣告 / life 生活	reading literacy 閱讀素養教育	planning and execution 規劃執行
passage 短文 / science 語言與溝通	life 生命教育	problem solving 解決問題
passage 短文 / social behavior 社會行為	disaster prevention 防災教育	planning and execution 規劃執行
passage 短文 / arts & literature 藝術與文學	morality 品德教育	physical and mental wellness 身心素質
news clip 新聞短片 / health & body 健康與身體	reading literacy 閱讀素養教育	physical and mental wellness 身心素質
website 網站 / entertainment 娛樂	technology 科技教育	planning and execution 規劃執行
poem 詩 / teens 青少年生活	morality 品德教育	self-advancement 自我精進
passage 短文 / famous people 名人	environment 環境教育	citizenship 公民意識

體裁 / 主題	議題	素養
passage 短文 / sports 運動	outdoor education 戶外教育	physical and mental wellness 身心素質
diary 日記 / daily routines 日常生活	reading literacy 閱讀素養教育	problem solving 解決問題
passage 短文 / health & body 健康與身體	reading literacy 閱讀素養教育	physical and mental wellness 身心素質
notice 通知 / life 生活	security 安全教育	planning and execution 規劃執行
passage 短文 / nature 自然	environment 環境教育	
passage 短文 / families & kinship terms 家庭與親屬關係	family education 家庭教育	interpersonal relationship 人際關係
table 表格 / health & body 健康與身體	reading literacy 閱讀素養教育	logical thinking 系統思考
line graph 折線圖 / Internet or technology 網路科技	technology 科技教育	information and technology literacy 科技資訊
Venn diagram 文氏圖 / animals 動物	life 生命教育	problem solving 解決問題
bar graph 長條圖 / environment 環境	environment 環境教育	problem solving 解決問題
pie chart 圓餅圖 / entertainment 娛樂		artistic appreciation 藝術涵養
table of contents 目錄 / language & communication 語言與溝通	information 資訊教育	expression 溝通表達
dictionary 字典 / animals 動物	life 生命教育	semiotics 符號運用
map 地圖 / culture 文化	indigenous education 原住民教育	cultural understanding 多元文化

體裁 / 主題	議題	素養
index 索引 / travel 旅遊	information 資訊教育	semiotics 符號運用
recipe 食譜 / culture 文化	multiculturalism 多元文化教育	cultural understanding 多元文化
website 網站 / career 職涯	career planning 生涯規劃教育	planning and execution 規劃執行
advertisement 廣告 / Internet or technology 網路科技	technology 科技教育	innovation and adaptation 創新應變
brochure 傳單 / nature 自然	outdoor education 戶外教育	teamwork 團隊合作
talk 演講 / plants 植物	information 資訊教育	expression 溝通表達
poem 詩 / life 生活	morality 品德教育	physical and mental wellness 身心素質
passage 短文 / famous place 有名景點	environment 環境教育	
magazine article 雜誌文章 / health & body 健康與身體	information 資訊教育	problem solving 解決問題
dialogue 對話 / gender equality 性別平等	gender equality 性別平等教育	interpersonal relationship 人際關係
table 表格 / families & kinship terms 家庭與親屬關係	family education 家庭教育	teamwork 團隊合作
timeline 時間軸 / Internet or technology 網路科技	technology 科技教育	information and technology literacy 科技資訊

Introduction

本套書共四冊，專為英語初學者設計，旨在**增進閱讀理解能力**並**提升閱讀技巧**。全套書符合 108 課綱要旨，強調**跨領域、生活化學習**，文章按照教育部公布的**九大核心素養**與 **19 項議題設計**撰寫，為讀者打造扎實的英語閱讀核心素養能力。

每冊內含 50 篇文章，主題包羅萬象，包括**文化、科學、自然、文學**等，內容以**日常生活常見體裁**寫成，舉凡**電子郵件、邀請函、廣告、公告、對話**皆收錄於書中，以多元主題及多變體裁，豐富讀者閱讀體驗，引導讀者從生活中學習，並將學習運用於生活。每篇文章之後設計**五道閱讀理解題**，依不同閱讀技巧重點精心撰寫，訓練統整、分析及應用所得資訊的能力，同時為日後的國中教育會考做準備。

Key Features 本書特色

1. 按文章難度分級，可依程度選用適合的級數

全套書難度不同，方便各程度的學生使用，以文章字數、高級字詞使用數、文法難度、句子長度分為一至四冊，如下方表格所示：

文章字數 （每篇）	國中 1200 字 （每篇）	國中 1201–2000 字 （每篇）	高中 7000 字 （3–5 級）（每篇）	文法	句子最長字數
Book 1 120–150	93%	7 字	3 字	國一	15 字
Book 2 150–180	86%	15 字	6 字	國二	18 字
Book 3 180–210	82%	30 字	7 字	國三	25 字
Book 4 210–250	75%	50 字	12 字	進階	28 字

2. 按文章難度分級，可依程度選用適合的級數

全書**主題多元**，有**青少年生活、家庭、娛樂、環境、健康、節慶、文化、動物、文學、旅遊**等，帶領讀者以英語探索知識、豐富生活，同時拉近學習與日常的距離。

3. 文章體裁豐富多樣

廣納各類生活中**常見的體裁**，包含**短文、詩篇、對話、廣告、傳單、新聞、短片、專欄**等，讓讀者學會閱讀多種體裁文章，將閱讀知識及能力應用於生活中。

4. 外師親錄課文朗讀 MP3

全書文章皆由專業外師錄製 MP3，示範正確發音，促進讀者聽力吸收，提升英文聽力與口說能力。

Structure of the Book | 本書架構

Unit 1 閱讀技巧 Reading Skills

本單元訓練讀者**理解文意**的基本技巧，內容包含：

❶ 明辨主題／歸納要旨 Subject Matter / Main Idea

主題指的是文章整體涵括的概念，**要旨**則是文章傳達的關鍵訊息，也就是作者想要講述的重點。一般而言，只要看前三句就能大略掌握文章的主題與要旨。

❷ 找出支持性細節／理解因果關係 Supporting Details / Cause and Effect

支持性細節就像是築起房屋的磚塊，幫助讀者逐步了解整篇文章要旨，**事實**、**描述**、**比較**、**舉例**都能是支持性細節的一種。

一起事件通常都有發生的原因與造成的結果，讀者可以從文章內的 **because of**（由於）、**as a result of**（因而）等片語找出原因，並從 **as a result**（結果，不加 of）、**resulting in**（因此）和 **so**（所以）等片語得知結果。

❸ 分辨事實與意見／做出推測 Fact or Opinion / Making Inferences

可以經其他資料來證實的稱為**事實**，他人主觀的想法或感覺則稱為**意見**。例如「World War II ended in 1945.」（第二次世界大戰在 1945 年結束）是事實，而「I hate war.」（我討厭戰爭）則屬於意見。

推測代表使用已知的資訊去推論出未知的事情，要推測文意，通常需要從文章各處得到線索。

Unit 2 | 字彙學習 Word Study

本單元訓練讀者擴充字彙量，並學會了解文章中的生字，內容包含：

① 同義詞與反義詞 Synonyms / Antonyms

在英文中有時兩字的意思相近，此時稱這兩字為**同義詞**；若兩字意思完全相反，則稱為**反義詞**。舉例來說，good（好）和 brilliant（很棒）的意思相近，為同義詞，但 good（好）和 bad（壞）的意思相反，故為反義詞。學習這些詞彙有助提升字彙量，並增進閱讀與寫作能力。

② 從上下文推測字義 Words In Context

遇到不會的英文字，就算是跟它大眼瞪小眼，也無法了解其字義，但若好好觀察此字的**上下文**，或許就能推敲出大略的字義。這項技巧十分重要，尤其有助讀者在閱讀文章時，即使遇到不會的生字，也能選出正確答案。

Unit 3 | 學習策略 Study Strategies

影像圖表與**參考資料**常會附在文章旁，幫助讀者獲得許多額外重點，本單元引導讀者善用文章中的不同素材來蒐集資訊，內容包含：

① 影像圖表 Visual Material

影像圖表可以將複雜資訊轉換成簡單的**表格、圖表、地圖**等，是閱讀時的最佳幫手。要讀懂圖表，首先要閱讀**圖表標題與單位**，接著觀察**數值**，只要理解圖表的架構，就能從中得到重要資訊。

② 參考資料 Reference Sources

參考資料像是**字典、書籍索引**等，一次呈現大量資訊，能訓練讀者自行追蹤所需重點的能力，並提升讀者對文章的整體理解。

Unit 4 | 綜合練習 Final Reviews

本單元綜合前三單元內容，幫助讀者回顧全書所學，並藉由文後綜合習題，來檢視自身吸收程度。

How to Use This Book?

1 多樣主題增添閱讀樂趣與知識

性別

文化

動物

09

» gender equality

Time to
Break the Rules!

1 **Blue is for boys and pink is for girls**—isn't that the rule? Well, maybe not.

⌃ Franklin Roosevelt wore white dress as a child in 1884.

2 This idea only became common in the 1950s. Before that, no one could agree on what colors were best for boys and girls. Some baby magazines even said pink for boys (because it is a stronger color) and blue for girls (because it is prettier). In fact, around 150 years ago, all young children—boys and girls—wore white dresses.

3 So why do we have this idea now? Our modern color rules are the result of big companies wanting to sell us things more easily.

38

Taiwan's First People

1 Taiwan is home to over 23 million people. A little over 2% (around 560,000) are Taiwanese aborigines. Taiwanese aborigines came to Taiwan thousands of years ago. They used to live all over Taiwan. But in the 1600s, people from China and Europe began coming to the island. They fought with the aborigines for control of the land. Now, Taiwanese aborigines mostly live on the island's east coast and in the central mountains.

⌃ Amis'

2 There are 16 different groups of Taiwanese aborigines. They all have their own customs, festivals, and language. The largest of these 16 groups is the Amis, with a little over 200,000 people. From the map, you can see the Amis live in the central part of Taiwan's east coast. The map also has information about other groups. By looking at the map, you can see where Taiwan's aboriginal groups live.

37

« Hippos have large teeth.

⌄ Hippos look funny with their big, round bodies.

Funny-Looking,
but Dangerous!

1 Hippos are large African mammals. They live in rivers and look quite funny with their little ears and big, round, gray bodies. But in fact, they are one of the world's most dangerous animals. Hippos get angry very easily. They have large teeth. And they can run really fast. Every year, they kill around 500 people in Africa.

2 Some people also say hippos sweat blood! Scary, right? Yes, if it were true. A hippo's sweat is red, but it isn't blood. It is actually a type of oil. This special oil protects a hippo's skin from the hot African sun.

3 I first saw the word hippo in a book about Africa. I had to look it up in a dictionary because I didn't know what it meant. I found the word on a page in the H section. Take a look at some of the other words on that page. They all start with the letters "hi–."

詩篇

邀請函

UNIT 1 🎧 12

12 Party Time

party hat

☆ party flag

candle

Time: Friday, April 24th, 2021, 4:00 – Saturday, April 25th, 2021, 11:00

Location: My house, the skate park, and Full Moon Pizza Restaurant

Created by: Billy Smith

Hi everyone!

1 I am going to have a big party for my thirteenth birthday on Friday. You can come back home with me after school. We can leave our school bags at my house. Then, we will go skating. If you don't have skates, don't worry. I have skates for you to borrow.

2 After that, we will get pizza. **Full Moon has the best pizza!** Please tell me what kind of pizza you like so I can call the restaurant and order it. If you don't like pizza, they have other things.

3 After that, you can come to my house and stay over. We are going to camp out in my garden. I have tents for you to use, but please bring your own sleeping bag. **It will be really fun!**

See you later!

Billy

038

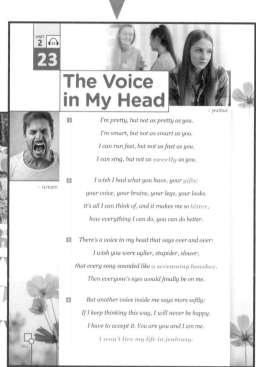

UNIT 2 🎧 23

23 The Voice in My Head

☆ jealous

☆ scream

1 *I'm pretty, but not as pretty as you.*
I'm smart, but not as smart as you.
I can run fast, but not as fast as you.
I can sing, but not as sweetly as you.

2 *I wish I had what you have, your gifts:*
your voice, your brains, your legs, your looks.
It's all I can think of, and it makes me so bitter,
how everything I can do, you can do better.

3 *There's a voice in my head that says over and over:*
I wish you were uglier, stupider, slower,
that every song sounded like a screaming banshee.
Then everyone's eyes would finally be on me.

4 *But another voice inside me says more softly:*
If I keep thinking this way, I will never be happy.
I have to accept it. You are you and I am me.
I won't live my life in jealousy.

052

網頁

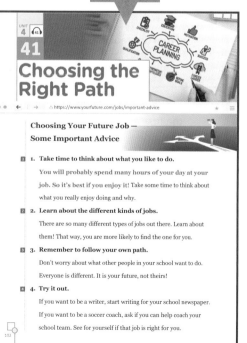

UNIT 4 🎧 41

41 Choosing the Right Path

CAREER PLANNING

🔒 https://www.yourfuture.com/jobs/important-advice

Choosing Your Future Job —
Some Important Advice

1 **1. Take time to think about what you like to do.**
You will probably spend many hours of your day at your job. So it's best if you enjoy it! Take some time to think about what you really enjoy doing and why.

2 **2. Learn about the different kinds of jobs.**
There are so many different types of jobs out there. Learn about them! That way, you are more likely to find the one for you.

3 **3. Remember to follow your own path.**
Don't worry about what other people in your school want to do. Everyone is different. It is your future, not theirs!

4 **4. Try it out.**
If you want to be a writer, start writing for your school newspaper. If you want to be a soccer coach, ask if you can help coach your school team. See for yourself if that job is right for you.

102

每篇文章後附五道閱讀理解題，
訓練培養九大閱讀技巧，包含：

_____ 1. **What is this reading mostly about?**
   a. Cultural bias.　　b. Face masks.
   c. Being rude.　　d. Getting a cold.

❶ 明辨主題

_____ 2. **What's the main idea of this reading?**
   a. Face masks mean different things in different cultures.
   b. We should all wear face masks at all times.
   c. It is easy to get sick when you visit a new country.
   d. Face masks are easier to find in some countries than others.

❷ 歸納要旨

_____ 1. **Which of the following is NOT true about the tripping jump challenge?**
   a. It takes three people to do it.
   b. It is very dangerous.
   c. It has been around for a long time.
   d. It began in America.

❸ 找出支持性細節

_____ 2. **Which of the following does NOT come from the tripping jump challenge, based on the reading?**
   a. Death.　　b. A headache.
   c. Back problems.　　d. Brain Damage.

❹ 理解因果關係

_____ 1. **How did Suzie feel when she saw her candy was not on the desk?**
   a. She felt surprised.　　b. She felt excited.
   c. She felt unhappy.　　d. She felt hungry.

_____ 2. **"Suddenly, we saw Suzie's candy on the desk." Is this a fact or the writer's opinion?**
   a. Fact.　　b. Opinion.

❺ 分辨事實與意見

_____ 3. **From the reading, what is probably TRUE about Tom?**
   a. He is lazy.　　b. He is afraid.
   c. He is honest.　　d. He is helpful.

❻ 做出推測

_____ 1. **Which of the following words means the same as "sweetly" in the first paragraph?**
   a. Badly.　　b. Beautifully.　　c. Loudly.　　d. Deliciously.

❼ 了解同義字

_____ 2. **What does the word "gift" mean in the second paragraph?**
   a. Something special that you were born with.
   b. Something you give to a friend for their birthday.
   c. Something that is cheap and easy to buy.
   d. Something that looks good but isn't real.

❽ 從上下文推測字義

_____ 3. **Which of these has the opposite meaning to "bitter" in the second paragraph?**
   a. Sharp.　　b. Angry.　　c. Happy.　　d. Pretty.

❾ 了解反義字

地圖

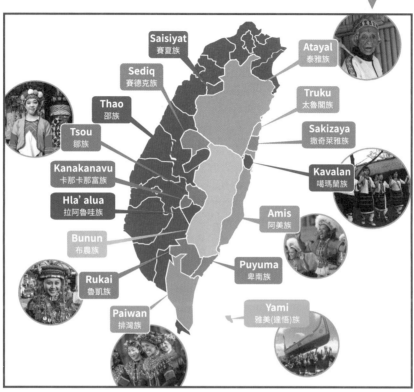

圖片

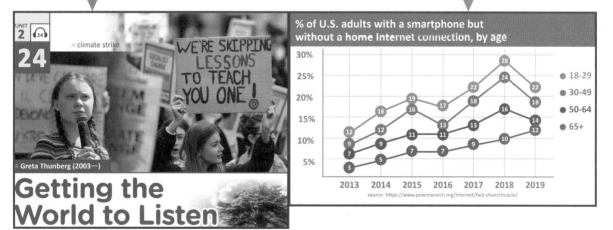

折線圖

UNIT
1

Reading Skills

This unit covers six key ideas to look for when reading an article, including subject matter, main idea(s), supporting details, cause and effect, inferences, and fact or opinion.

In this unit, you will learn to recognize what a text is mainly about, understand how an author feels about a topic, make assumptions based on information, and observe how details can be used to support main ideas.

01
A Strange New Language

:-)

influencer

go viral

2,215,600,780

9,036,259   1,188,691

You're ugly

QWERTY
ASDF

troll

1   The Internet is a strange place. It sometimes feels like its own country with its own special language. To help you learn that language, here are some common Internet words and their meanings:

2 **Influencer:** A person with many fans on social media. *(e.g., "It seems like these days everyone wants to be an Instagram influencer.")*

3 **Hashtag:** The # symbol followed by a word or phrase. People often use hashtags to indicate the topic of a post. *(e.g., "I just bought some metal straws. #savetheplanet")*

4 **Go viral:** If a video, picture, or story goes viral, it spreads quickly on the Internet. (e.g., "Johnny's dance video went viral. It already has over 1,000,000 views!")

@

5 **Troll:** Someone rude or mean on the Internet. *(e.g., "Stop writing bad comments about my photos. You're such a troll!")*

6 **Netizen:** Anyone who uses the Internet often. *(e.g., "Taiwanese netizens love watching food videos on YouTube.")*

QUESTION

_____1. **What is the reading about?**
- a. Popular Internet videos.
- b. Common Internet words.
- c. Rude people on the Internet.
- d. Internet users in Taiwan.

_____2. **What is the main idea of the reading?**
- a. There are many words you should know if you want to talk about the Internet.
- b. Many people want to become popular on Instagram.
- c. Some online videos spread very quickly.
- d. People often use hashtags to mark the topic of their post.

_____3. **What is the third paragraph about?**
- a. Where to buy metal straws.
- b. Where the symbol # comes from.
- c. The meaning of the word "hashtag."
- d. How to save the planet.

_____4. **What is the main idea of the fifth paragraph?**
- a. You shouldn't write mean things about people's photos.
- b. The Internet can be a dangerous place.
- c. You should not worry about Internet trolls.
- d. "Troll" refers to someone who is rude on the Internet.

_____5. **You found something in a dictionary:**

> **binge-watch** (v.)
>
> Watching all of a TV show in a short time.
>
> e.g., "I binge-watched all 4 seasons of *Riverdale* on Saturday."

What is this about?
- a. The show *Riverdale*.
- b. The meaning of "binge-watch."
- c. What I did on Saturday.
- d. Cool new TV shows.

02

Cultural Differences Behind the Mask

Rob: Achoo!

Constance: Yikes. It sounds like you are getting a cold. Would you like to have one of my face masks?

5   **Rob:** Thank you, but what's the point? I'm already sick.

Constance: That's the most important time to wear a mask! You don't want to infect other people, right?

Rob: Wait, so you're saying all those people wearing face masks here are already sick?

10   **Constance:** Yes. It's part of the local culture here. It's considered rude to be sick in public and not wear a mask.

Rob: That makes a lot of sense now that I think of it. In the West, almost no one wears them. What's more, some people think it's rude to talk to someone if you cover your face.

Constance: So would you like to wear one?

Rob: Of course! I don't want to be rude. After all, the best thing about living in a new country is learning from another culture.

⌃ covering one's face

QUESTION

_____1. **What is this reading mostly about?**
   a. Cultural bias.   b. Face masks.
   c. Being rude.   d. Getting a cold.

_____2. **What's the main idea of this reading?**
   a. Face masks mean different things in different cultures.
   b. We should all wear face masks at all times.
   c. It is easy to get sick when you visit a new country.
   d. Face masks are easier to find in some countries than others.

_____3. **What is the last line mostly about?**
   a. People can be rude sometimes.   b. Face masks.
   c. Living in a new place.   d. Infection.

_____4. **What is the first dialogue mostly about?**
   a. Being sick.   b. Living in a new place.
   c. Local culture.   d. Learning from other cultures.

_____5. **When Rob speaks for the fourth time, what is the main idea he expresses?**
   a. The weather is worse in the West.
   b. It is hard to find a face mask in the West.
   c. Face masks mean something different in the West.
   d. Most people are scared of getting sick in the West.

03 Can Men Do Hula?

posted: 2020/12/24 13:43

1   Do you know about the hula dance from Hawaii? Usually, people think hula dancers are women in grass skirts. But men can do it, too!

2   In the past, it was very important for men to do the hula well. If you were a good hula dancer, you could be a good fighter. All the men wanted to be the best fighter. So they did a lot of training to become fast and strong.

3   Even today, Hawaiian men dance the hula. But they don't go to the gym for training. They do the same things that people did in the past. They swim in the sea and run along the beach with heavy rocks. They even climb to the top of coconut trees.

4   Today's male hula dancers don't want to fight. They want to remember the old ways of their grandfathers and great-grandfathers. Hula improves their bodies and also their minds.

« grass skirt

≫ gym

QUESTION

_____ 1. **What is the reading about?**
- a. Going to the gym.
- b. A Hawaiian dance.
- c. People fighting.
- d. A beautiful beach.

_____ 2. **What does the writer say in the first paragraph?**
- a. Men usually cannot do hula well.
- b. Not many people know the hula.
- c. You should do the hula in a skirt.
- d. Not only women do the hula.

_____ 3. **What is the main idea of the second paragraph?**
- a. Hula dancers were not allowed to fight.
- b. Some men thought hula was only for women.
- c. There used to be big hula competitions.
- d. Hula helped men become good at fighting.

_____ 4. **What is the third paragraph about?**
- a. How hula dancers train today.
- b. How hula dancers trained in the past.
- c. How to get better at running.
- d. How to get better at swimming.

_____ 5. **What does the writer say in the last paragraph?**
- a. Hula is too hard for older people.
- b. Today, men dance better than before.
- c. Hula dancers do not fight any more.
- d. Learning hula only helps your body.

≫ coconut tree

» quarantine at home

Staying Safe During COVID-19

1   There are many types of coronavirus. Some are not serious, like a common cold, and some are dangerous. The COVID-19 virus enters our bodies and then grows and makes us sick. COVID-19 goes from person to person easily and can make us so sick that we could die.

≫ It is possible to catch COVID-19 from touching something that a sick person had touched.

2   We can get COVID-19 from being too close to someone who has it and sneezes or coughs on us. It is also possible to catch it from touching something that a sick person has touched. If we have it on our hands and then touch our face, we can catch it this way too. In order to stop people from catching the virus, doctors say we should wash our hands often and not get too close to each other.

3   We must remember to be safe now and prepare for the next time there is a dangerous virus.

≫ washing hands

≫ coughing

≫ sneezing

QUESTION

_____1. **What is the reading about?**
   a. COVID-19 is serious and we should try to avoid catching it.
   b. Other coronaviruses are worse than COVID-19.
   c. Touching your face can give you COVID-19.
   d. Crowded places are very dangerous if you have COVID-19.

_____2. **What is the first paragraph about?**
   a. COVID-19 enters our bodies.
   b. The common cold is one type of coronavirus.
   c. COVID-19 is a serious type of coronavirus.
   d. We can catch COVID-19 very easily.

_____3. **What would be another good title for this reading?**
   a. Getting a common cold.   b. Touching sick people.
   c. Beating a serious virus.   d. Being ready for the future.

_____4. **What is the second paragraph mostly about?**
   a. How we can catch COVID-19.   b. The things doctors say.
   c. The things on our faces.   d. Why we cough.

_____5. **What does the last paragraph tell us?**
   a. Stop preparing.
   b. Another virus is coming.
   c. Be ready if another virus comes.
   d. Help COVID-19 patients.

» female blue manakin

» male blue manakins

With a Little Help From My Friends

Tuesday Truths

with Claire Smith

1 Isn't it strange how even the silliest thing can make you realize something important?

2 A few days ago I saw a funny video online of a little blue bird from Brazil. To get a girlfriend, this bird needs the help of two friends. Every day, they practice a difficult dance until it is perfect. Then they do the dance for a female bird. If the female thinks the dance was good enough, she will let the leader be her boyfriend.

3 At first I laughed at the funny birds and their silly dance. But then I remembered all the times my friends helped me do something difficult. I realized how great it is to have friends who will help you when you need it most.

4 So, my truth for this Tuesday is this: be thankful for your friends because they make the impossible possible!

 # QUESTION

_____ 1. **Which of these sentences is the reading's main idea?**

   a. "A few days ago I saw a funny video online. . . ."

   b. "At first I laughed at the funny birds and their silly dance."

   c. "Every day, they practice a difficult dance. . . ."

   d. ". . . be thankful for your friends because they make the impossible possible."

_____ 2. **What is the second paragraph about?**

   a. A bird from Brazil.   b. How to get a girlfriend.

   c. A famous leader.   d. How to be a good dancer.

_____ 3. **What is the third paragraph about?**

   a. A funny joke.   b. An important truth.

   c. A sad story.   d. A big lie.

_____ 4. **Which of these could be another title for the article?**

   a. Making Friends on Your First Day of School

   b. Is Your Best Friend a Bad Friend?

   c. You Can Do It If You Have Good Friends

   d. Online Friends: The New Normal?

_____ 5. **One of Claire's readers enjoyed her article and wrote her an email.**

 To: Claire Smith
From: Jenny Tsai
Subject: Tuesday Truths

Hi Claire,

I read your column about the dancing birds last Tuesday. It was such a fun read. After I read it I went online and watched the video. It's so cute! But really, I'm writing to thank you. I always thought I could do everything by myself. Now I understand how important my friends are. You taught me an important lesson. Thank you so much!

Your biggest fan,
Jenny

What is the main point of Jenny's email?

   a. To say how much of a big fan she is.   b. To tell Claire about her friends.

   c. To thank Claire for her wise words.   d. To say how cute the video is.

06

Goodbye, Miss James!

≫ raising one's hand

Dear Miss James,

1 I am so sad to hear that you are leaving next week. I will miss you very much. You taught me so many important things this semester. You taught me how to write better, how to use many new words, and how to speak correctly. But more importantly, you taught me how to believe in myself.

2 Last year I was very shy in English class. I didn't like to raise my hand because I was afraid I would make a mistake. But you taught me that trying is what's important. And if I make a mistake, it doesn't matter because I can learn from it and get better.

3 I am a lot more confident now because of you. I hope when you return to the United States, you won't forget our class. We will all be thinking of you.

4 Best wishes,

Lilly,

Class 2A

≫ shy

QUESTION

_____1. **What kind of student was Lilly before Miss James became her teacher?**
    a. Shy.   **b.** Confident.   **c.** Lazy.   **d.** Bored.

_____2. **Which of the following did Miss James NOT teach Lilly?**
    a. How to write better.   **b.** How to speak correctly.
    c. How to believe in herself.   **d.** How to make new friends.

_____3. **Why is Miss James leaving?**
    a. She is returning to the United States.
    b. She is moving to a different local school.
    c. She is having a baby.
    d. She needs to take care of her sick mom.

_____4. **Why didn't Lilly like raising her hand last year?**
    a. She didn't like Miss James.
    b. She didn't like English class.
    c. She was afraid of making a mistake.
    d. She was too tired to move.

_____5. **Below is Miss James's reply to Lilly.**

> Dear Lilly,
>
> Thank you so much for your kind words.
> I'm so happy you are not afraid to raise your hand anymore. You are
> a great student. I know if you keep being brave and trying hard, your
> English will get better and better!
> I had a great time teaching Class 2A. Of course I won't forget you all!
> Best wishes from the USA!
>
> Miss James

What does Miss James say Lilly should do if she wants to get better at English?
    a. Review her work at home.
    b. Continue to be brave and try hard.
    c. Find an American friend.
    d. Ask her parents for help with her homework.

07 A Challenge to Good Sense

Sandra: Hey, Louie! What's up?

Louie: Oh, hi, Sandra.

Sandra: You look upset. Is something wrong?

Louie: My brother is in the hospital.

5 **Sandra:** Jack? Why?

Louie: He got hurt by the tripping jump challenge.

Sandra: What's that?

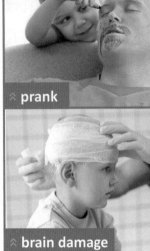

≫ prank

≫ brain damage

Louie: It's a stupid, dangerous new prank from America.

Sandra: How does it work?

10 **Louie:** Two people trick a third person into standing between them. They say they want to make a video of all three people jumping together. When the person in the middle jumps, the other two kick his legs out so he falls flat on his back.

Sandra: That sounds really dangerous. And Jack fell for it?

15 **Louie:** Yeah. These two "friends" of his did it to him. Now his back is badly hurt. Other people landed on their heads and got brain damage. Two kids died from it!

Sandra: That's terrible! I hope Jack gets better soon.

Louie: He should, thanks. I just hope he's more careful next time.

Q UESTION

_____ 1. **Which of the following is NOT true about the tripping jump challenge?**

a. It takes three people to do it.

b. It is very dangerous.

c. It has been around for a long time.

d. It began in America.

_____ 2. **Which of the following does NOT come from the tripping jump challenge, based on the reading?**

a. Death.   b. A headache.

c. Back problems.   d. Brain Damage.

_____ 3. **Why is Louie upset?**

a. Because his brother is badly hurt.

b. Because he did the tripping jump challenge.

c. Because Sandra doesn't know about the tripping jump challenge.

d. Because people died doing the tripping jump challenge.

_____ 4. **What does Sandra think about the tripping jump challenge?**

a. She thinks it's funny.   b. She wants to try it.

c. She is bored by it.   d. She thinks it's terrible.

_____ 5. **Which of the pictures below shows what happened to Louie's brother Jack?**

a.   b.   c.   d.

(cc by Anonymous Spanish Students)

08

Talking With Animals

1   Is your little brother a terrible copycat? Do you often smell a rat when your friend tells you a story? Is it raining cats and dogs outside? English has many animal sayings. But what do they mean? And where do they come from?

2 **Copycat:** Kittens learn how to be adults by copying their mother cat. If you copy how someone dresses or acts, you are just like a little kitten. You are a copycat!

3 **Smell a rat:** In the past, rats were everywhere. And they often spread diseases. Dogs could smell rats and chase them away. Do you think someone is spreading lies or cheating? Then you are like a dog smelling a dirty rat!

4 **Raining cats and dogs:** A long time ago, another word for waterfall was "**catadupe**." Over time this became "**cats and dogs**." So "it's raining cats and dogs" really means "it's raining waterfalls" (that is, A LOT!).

It's raining cats and dogs

» kitten

QUESTION

⩘ waterfall

_____1. **Which of these is TRUE about kittens?**

    a. They spread disease.   **b.** They can't smell very well.

    c. They like the rain.   **d.** They copy their mother.

_____2. **What did the word "catadupe" mean?**

    a. Waterfall.   **b.** A dirty rat.

    c. A mother cat.   **d.** Heavy rain.

_____3. **What might cause someone to call you a copycat?**

    a. Not covering your mouth when you cough.

    b. Wearing the same clothes as your friend.

    c. Forgetting your umbrella on a rainy day.

    d. Getting a cat instead of a dog.

_____4. **Why do we use the words "cats and dogs" in the phrase "It's raining cats and dogs"?**

    a. Cats and dogs are popular pets these days.

    b. People used cats and dogs to hunt rats in the past.

    c. The word "catadupe" changed to "cats and dogs" over time.

    d. Cats and dogs know when it's going to rain.

_____5. **In which of these pictures is someone smelling a rat?**

    a.

    b.

    c.

    d.

» gender equality

Time to Break the Rules!

1   **Blue is for boys and pink is for girls**—isn't that the rule? Well, maybe not.

2   This idea only became common in the 1950s. Before that, no one could agree on what colors were best for boys and girls. Some baby magazines even said pink for boys (because it is a stronger color) and blue for

⌃ Franklin Roosevelt wore white dress as a child in 1884.

girls (because it is prettier). In fact, around 150 years ago, all young children—boys and girls—wore white dresses.

3   So why do we have this idea now? Our modern color rules are the result of big companies wanting to sell us things more easily.

If you are a girl and you see something pink, you think "Ah! This thing is right for me." And you are more likely to buy it.

4 Of course, there is nothing wrong with boys liking pink or girls liking blue. When it comes to colors, it is OK to break the rules!

» gender stereotypes

QUESTION

_____ 1. **When did the idea "blue is for boys and pink is for girls" become common?**
   a. One hundred and fifty years ago.
   b. In the last 50 years.
   c. In the 1950s.
   d. In the 2000s.

_____ 2. **Which of the following is TRUE about what people wore 150 years ago?**
   a. All young girls wore blue pants.
   b. Young boys wore white dresses.
   c. Young children never wore white.
   d. All young children wore white shirts.

_____ 3. **In the past, why did some magazines think boys should wear pink?**
   a. It is a strong color.   b. It is easy to clean.
   c. It makes people feel happy.   d. It reminds people of flowers.

_____ 4. **Where do our modern color rules come from?**
   a. Young people breaking old rules.
   b. Old magazines telling people what to wear.
   c. People wanting to make their babies look cute.
   d. Big companies wanting to sell people things more easily.

_____ 5. **When girls see something pink in a store, what do they often think?**
   a. That thing is just for boys.   b. That thing is right for them.
   c. That thing is not for children.   d. That thing is too expensive.

Making the Right Choice

Jess: What's wrong, little brother?

Matt: My friends want me to go to the night market with them tonight. But I really should stay at home and study for my test.

Jess: So what are you going to do?

5 **Matt:** I don't know. All my friends are going. They said I should forget my test and go out and have fun with them.

Jess: I see. It can be hard to say no to your friends.

Matt: Yes. I'm afraid that if I stay at home and study, they'll stop wanting to be friends with
10 me.

Jess: Is your test important?

Matt: Yes, I really need to get a good grade.

Jess: Then here's my advice. Don't be afraid to do what's best for yourself, even if your
15 friends disagree.

Matt: But what if they stop being friends with me?

Jess: Then they weren't very good friends.

Matt: I guess you're right. Thanks, Jess.

⌃ a good grade

⌃ night market

QUESTION

_____1. **What are Matt's friends doing tonight?**
- **a.** Going to a baseball game.
- **b.** Staying at home.
- **c.** Going to the night market.
- **d.** Going to a birthday party.

_____2. **Which of these is TRUE?**
- **a.** Matt's friends don't want him to go with them.
- **b.** Matt needs to study for an important test.
- **c.** Matt wants Jess to go with them.
- **d.** Matt thinks Jess's advice is bad.

_____3. **What does Matt think will happen if he doesn't go with his friends?**
- **a.** Jess will go instead of him.
- **b.** His parents will be mad at him.
- **c.** His friends will stop being friends with him.
- **d.** He'll fail his test.

_____4. **What advice does Jess give to Matt?**
- **a.** He should do what's best for himself.
- **b.** He should do what his friends tell him to do.
- **c.** He should ask his parents what they think.
- **d.** He shouldn't worry so much about his grades.

_____5. **After talking to his big sister, Matt** **spoke with his friends using their group chat. Here's their conversation.**

 Hi Matt, are you ready for the night market?

Sorry, guys. I think I'm going to stay at home tonight. I need to study.

 Come on, Matt. We're your friends. What's more important?

You're important, but my test is important, too.

 OK, Matt. We understand. There's always next time.

You guys are the best!

What was the effect of Matt's talk with his sister?
- **a.** He went out with his friends and didn't study for his test.
- **b.** He told friends that he didn't like them anymore.
- **c.** He didn't go out with his friends, but they are still friends.
- **d.** He didn't go out with his friends, and they stopped being his friend.

≫ traffic jam

Afternoon Traffic Report

1   I'm Lacey Bridgeman and this is the traffic news. Drivers can expect jams around Green Street this afternoon. A bus hit a tree at 11:30 this morning, so there are long lines of traffic. It's looking pretty terrible there right now. No one was badly hurt, but the bus is still blocking the street. If you have to drive in this area, you should use Jackson Road instead. Luckily, police say the traffic jam should be over before 5:00 p.m. tonight.

2   It's also very busy around Central Market. **There's a food festival outside, so several roads are closed.** I'm afraid it's not possible to drive in this area at all today. The best thing to do is park your car on Bird Street. From there, you can walk to the festival or take a free bus. It stops near Central Market and is running between 12:00 p.m. and 10:00 p.m. today. And now let's hear the weather report. . . .

» car accident

QUESTION

_____1. **What do we learn about the results of the accident?**
  a. Jackson Road is blocked.
  b. The bus driver was seriously hurt.
  c. Police are trying to move the bus.
  d. The roads will be clear by the evening.

_____2. **Which of these is an opinion?**
  a. "It's looking pretty terrible."
  b. "A bus hit a tree."
  c. "No one was badly hurt."
  d. "The bus is still blocking the street."

_____3. **What do we learn about the food festival?**
  a. Millions of people will visit.
  b. It costs nothing to enter.
  c. You can only visit on foot.
  d. It will last for three days.

_____4. **"There's a food festival outside, so several roads are closed."**
  Is this a fact or the writer's opinion?
  a. Opinion.   b. Fact.

_____5. **Which sign might you see on Bird Street today?**

a.
> **Buses to Central Market**
> **EVERY 30 MINUTES**
> **FROM NOON TO 10PM**

b.
> **Buses to Central Market**
> **EVERY 30 MINUTES**
> **FROM NOON TO 8PM**

c.
> **Buses to Green Market**
> **EVERY 30 MINUTES**
> **FROM NOON TO 10PM**

d.
> **CANNOT**
> **PARK HERE**

« traffic light

Party Time

party hat

candle

⌃ party flag

Time: Friday, April 24th, 2021, 4:00 − Saturday, April 25th, 2021, 11:00

Location: My house, the skate park, and Full Moon Pizza Restaurant

Created by: Billy Smith

Hi everyone!

1   I am going to have a big party for my thirteenth birthday on Friday. You can come back home with me after school. We can leave our school bags at my house. Then, we will go skating. If you don't have skates, don't worry. I have skates for you to borrow.

2   After that, we will get pizza. **Full Moon has the best pizza!** Please tell me what kind of pizza you like so I can call the restaurant and order it. If you don't like pizza, they have other things.

3   After that, you can come to my house and stay over. We are going to camp out in my garden. I have tents for you to use, but please bring your own sleeping bag. **It will be really fun!**

See you later!

Billy

QUESTION

_____1. **"Full Moon has the best pizza!" Is this a fact or the writer's opinion?**

    a. Fact.   b. Opinion.

_____2. **"It will be really fun!" Is this a fact or the writer's opinion?**

    a. Fact.   b. Opinion.

_____3. **From the reading, what is most likely TRUE about Billy?**

    a. He doesn't like camping.   b. He likes pizza.

    c. He is a very good student.   d. Billy sleeps in his garden.

_____4. **Which of these statements is a fact?**

    a. The party will be really fun.

    b. Billy has skates for his friends to use.

    c. Full Moon has the best pizza.

    d. The party will be big.

_____5. **Which of these things will NOT happen at Billy's party?**

    a.

    b.

    c.

    d.

13

Don't Be a Follower

⌃ leader ⌃ followers

1   Hello. My name is Tom. This is my speech about not being a follower. Last year, I was playing fidget spinners with my friend. We stood in the classroom and were playing happily together. **Suddenly, we saw Suzie's candy on the desk.** There was no one around. My friend told me to take Suzie's candy and eat it. I knew it was bad, but I followed what he said. I took it and ate it.

2   When Suzie saw her candy was gone, she cried. I felt so bad. I listened to my friend and didn't think about it myself. After that, I went to my school bag and took some of my own candy. I gave it to Suzie and said sorry for taking hers. She said it was OK. She thought my candy was better than hers. Now, I will always remember not to be a follower and think before doing something. Thank you for listening.

QUESTION

_____1. **How did Suzie feel when she saw her candy was not on the desk?**
   a. She felt surprised.   b. She felt excited.
   c. She felt unhappy.   d. She felt hungry.

_____2. **"Suddenly, we saw Suzie's candy on the desk." Is this a fact or the writer's opinion?**
   a. Fact.   b. Opinion.

_____3. **From the reading, what is probably TRUE about Tom?**
   a. He is lazy.   b. He is afraid.
   c. He is honest.   d. He is helpful.

_____4. **Which of these is an opinion?**
   a. "We stood in the classroom."
   b. "She thought my candy was better than hers."
   c. "When Suzie saw her candy was gone, she cried."
   d. "I gave it to Suzie and said sorry for taking hers."

_____5. **From the reading, which of these is probably NOT true?**
   a. Tom's friend knows Suzie.
   b. Tom and Suzie are friends.
   c. Tom's friend is Suzie's teacher.
   d. The three people are in the same class.

» fidget spinner

Happy New—*Shhh!*

1   Say the words "Happy New Year" and you'll probably think of fireworks, parties, and cheers. But not in Bali, Indonesia. There, the people spend the first day of each new year in peace and quiet.

2   Its name is *Nyepi*, or Silent Day. For 24 hours, no one can leave their house, make loud noises, or use electricity or fire. Many people also don't eat anything all day. The idea is to clean your body and mind before you begin the new year.

3   Everyone must treat *Nyepi* seriously, even tourists. Only special police can be out on the streets. They are there to make sure no one breaks the rules!

≫ On the eve of *Nyepi*, people will have grand parade with statues called *Ogoh-Ogoh*.

≫ A deserted Balinese street during *Nyepi* (cc by Davidelit)

4   *Nyepi* might not sound like much fun. But if you can make it through the day, you'll get a surprise. **Because all lights are off during *Nyepi*, at night you can clearly see millions of stars in the sky!** To me, that's way better than fireworks!

Q UESTION

_____1. **Which of these is an opinion?**
   a. "In Bali, people spend the first day of each year in peace and quiet."
   b. "Everyone must treat *Nyepi* seriously."
   c. "For 24 hours, no one can leave their house. "
   d. "*Nyepi* might not sound like much fun."

_____2. **Which of these do people probably do on *Nyepi*?**
   a. Watch TV at home.
   b. Walk the dog on the street.
   c. Do puzzle at home with family.
   d. Practice singing out loud.

_____3. **What should you do if you are on vacation in Bali during *Nyepi*?**
   a. Stay inside and be quiet.   b. Go to the beach.
   c. Take photos with the special police.   d. Set off fireworks.

_____4. **What can you guess about the writer?**
   a. He thinks the special police are all bad people.
   b. He thinks Chinese New Year is better than *Nyepi*.
   c. He enjoys being quiet for a long time.
   d. He likes stars more than fireworks.

_____5. **"Because all lights are off during *Nyepi*, at night you can clearly see millions of stars in the sky!" Is this a fact or the writer's opinion?**
   a. Fact.   b. Opinion.

Making Shadows Come to Life

1 Some people tell stories with words. Others tell stories with pictures. But did you know that you can tell stories with shadows?

2 Shadow play is a unique kind of storytelling. It began in China thousands of years ago. The storyteller sits behind a white paper screen and behind the screen is a light. When the storyteller holds up a puppet—a paper person or animal—its shadow appears on the screen. A good storyteller can make these shadows run, jump, fly, or even fight! Shadow play is always very exciting to watch!

⌃ shadow-play master / puppeteer

3 Shadow play is different from country to country. **In China, shadow plays are often about kings, queens, and heroes.** In Greece, however, they are often about common people and are very, very funny.

4 Sadly, there aren't many shadow-play masters left today. **So you should try to see a show before this kind of storytelling is gone forever.**

» puppets in Greece

QUESTION

_____1. **Which of these is the writer's opinion?**
  a. "Shadow play began in China thousands of years ago."
  b. "Shadow play is different from country to country."
  c. "There aren't many shadow-play masters left today."
  d. "Shadow play is always very exciting to watch."

_____2. **"In China, shadow plays are often about kings, queens, and heroes." Is this a fact or the writer's opinion?**
  a. Fact.   b. Opinion.

_____3. **In the final paragraph, the writer says, "So you should try to see a show before this kind of storytelling is gone forever." Is that a fact or the writer's opinion?**
  a. Fact.   b. Opinion.

_____4. **Which of the following does the writer wish?**
  a. That there were more shadow-play masters working today.
  b. That more shadow plays were about common people.
  c. That shadow plays were more exciting.
  d. That fewer people knew about shadow play.

_____5. **Which of the following can we guess from the second paragraph?**
  a. You can have a shadow play without any light.
  b. Only Chinese people can perform shadow plays.
  c. You need a lot of skill to be a good shadow-play storyteller.
  d. Many people find shadow plays boring to watch.

» germs

⌃ coughing into one's elbow

No More Sick Days!

Mr. Green: Where's Max today?

James: He's sick, Mr. Green. He has a bad cold.

Mr. Green: Not again! Someone is sick every week in this class. Lisa, weren't you sick last week?

Lisa: Yes, and both James and Ryan were sick the week before that.

Mr. Green: OK. This has got to stop. Next week, we need to make some changes.

James: What kind of changes?

Mr. Green: Well, I often see students coughing into their hands. Can anyone tell me why that's not the best thing to do?

Lisa: Because the germs get on your hands and then onto anything you touch.

Mr. Green: Right. So, let's all agree to cough into our elbows. That way we won't spread our germs around the classroom.

Class: Agreed!

Lisa: Oh! Mr. Green! We could also wash our hands with soap before coming into class.

Mr. Green: Great idea, Lisa. Can we all agree to that?

Class: Agreed!

Mr. Green: Good. Hopefully from now on, we'll have fewer sick students.

» hand wash / liquid soap

⌃ washing hands with soap

QUESTION

_____1. **What is the reading mainly about?**
   a. What to do if you have a cold.
   b. How to avoid getting sick.
   c. How to wash your hands correctly.
   d. How germs make people sick.

_____2. **Who was sick last week?**
   a. Max.
   b. Mr. Green.
   c. Lisa.
   d. James and Ryan.

_____3. **What does Mr. Green think is making students get sick?**
   a. Students washing their hands before coming into class.
   b. Students coughing into their elbows.
   c. Students taking time off school.
   d. Students coughing into their hands.

_____4. **Which of the following is a fact?**
   a. "Someone is sick every week in this class."
   b. "Next semester, we need to make some changes."
   c. "Great idea, Lisa."
   d. "Hopefully from now on, we'll have fewer sick students."

_____5. **Below is a line chart Mr. Green drew of how many sick students there were each week.**

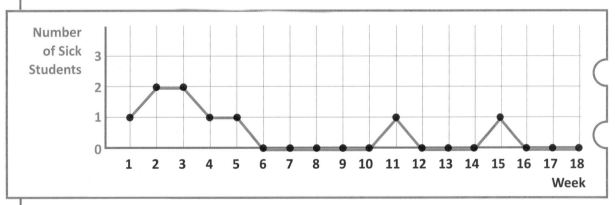

In the reading, the class agreed to make some changes.
When did they most likely start to make those changes?
   a. Week 1.
   b. Week 16.
   c. Week 6.
   d. Week 10.

17

Everything Must Go!

≫ flea market

≫ secondhand clothes

1   This year's summer student sale will happen next Saturday. Need a hot plate for your room? Or maybe you're looking to buy some used books for your classes? Now is your chance to get what you need. And even better: you can save some money while doing it!

2   The summer student sale is over 15 years old now. It started with a small group of international students. These students wanted to sell things they didn't need before they returned home. Now, the sale has grown into a very big event at the school.

3   Anyone can come and sell their goods. And you can sell almost anything, whether it's a bag or an old comic book. There will also be food and drinks on sale.

4   Don't miss it!

Time: 9:00 a.m. – 3:30 p.m.

Place: In front of the Main Student Building

Note: If you want to set up a selling table, **please email Mr. Lin before Saturday at mikelin4464@hotmail.com.**

QUESTION

_____1. **What is the second paragraph mostly about?**

    a. Items sold at the student sale.

    b. The history of the student sale.

    c. The cost of taking part in the student sale.

    d. The size of the student sale.

_____2. **Which of the following will you mostly NOT find at the student sale?**

    a. Book bag.   b. Pet.   c. Food and drink.   d. Comic books.

_____3. **What is the main idea of the third paragraph?**

    a. The sale is open to anyone and almost anything.

    b. You can find comic books at the sale.

    c. There will be food and drinks at the sale.

    d. The sale will happen on Saturday.

_____4. **What is probably TRUE about Mr. Lin?**

    a. He went to every summer student sale.

    b. He is interested in selling some of his comics.

    c. He is excited about the sale and can't wait.

    d. He is a school worker and he is in charge of the sale.

_____5. **Joey went to the student sale three years ago. Which one is the picture he took?**

a.

b.

c.

d.

18

The Strongest Webs on Earth

1 You might be scared of spiders. But did you know that spiders are like little engineers? Their webs are quite strong. How strong? Some studies show when you have enough spiderwebs, they could be five times stronger than metal. And think of how small they are. If a spider were our size, its web could stop an airplane.

2 Some people are trying to make spiderwebs even stronger. Students at the University of Trento are working with spiders' silk. They want to change the spider so it will make stronger silk. This means their webs would be stronger, too. The work could have uses

« Spiderman   ⌃ spiderweb

in the real world. Think of clothes made from spiders' silk. **They would feel so comfortable and they would be quite strong.** Maybe very soon, they will make special clothes for police. Not even bullets can shoot through these clothes. It would make the police as strong as Superman!

⌃ bullet

⌃ bulletproof vest

QUESTION

_____1. **What is the first paragraph about?**
   a. The size of spiders.   b. Spiderwebs.
   c. Airplanes.   d. Engineers.

_____2. **What is the main idea of the second paragraph?**
   a. Spiders' silk has uses in the real world.
   b. Students at the University of Trento are working hard.
   c. We can make clothes from spiders' silk.
   d. Spiderwebs are quite strong.

_____3. **What's another thing that we could probably use spiders' silk to make?**
   a. Glasses.   b. Computers.   c. Swords.   d. Rope.

_____4. **Which of the following is TRUE about spiderwebs?**
   a. Spiderwebs are very heavy.
   b. People can use spiderwebs to build a car.
   c. Spiderwebs can be stronger than metal.
   d. Spiderwebs are quite dangerous.

_____5. **"They would feel so comfortable and they would be quite strong." Is this a fact or the writer's opinion?**
   a. Fact.   b. Opinion.

^ long queue

Shopping That Goes Too Far

1   When a disaster happens, everyone starts to think the same way. They think: What if all the stores close? What if I don't have food anymore? What if I can't find medicine in two weeks? Many of these people then decide to go out and buy whatever they can. They might even buy things they don't even need. Some call this "stocking up." Others call it "panic buying."

2   But there's a big problem with panic buying. **Stores don't carry enough stock for everyone to buy so much.** This means that only some people are able to stock up. Others miss out, because there's nothing to buy when they get to the store. In times like these, it is panic buying that is the problem—not the disaster.

3   You will probably never experience a disaster. But if you do, buy only the things you need. That way, other people will also get their share.

QUESTION

_____1. **What is the main idea of the last paragraph?**
a. Do not panic buy.
b. You may experience a disaster.
c. Think about what you need.
d. It is hard to think about other people.

_____2. **What is the first paragraph about?**
a. Stores running out of items.
b. Where people can find medicine.
c. What people do in a disaster.
d. What you shouldn't do in a disaster.

_____3. **"Stores don't carry enough stock for everyone to buy so much."**
Is this a fact or the writer's opinion?
a. Fact.   b. Opinion.

_____4. **What is another item that people probably panic buy during a disaster?**
a. Pets.   b. CDs.   c. Books.   d. Cooking oil.

_____5. **John took a picture of people panic buying after an earthquake. Which of the following could be the picture he took?**

a.

b.

c.

d.

⌄ desert island (cc by Emperor Deathsaur)

Wild Boys

⌃ William Golding (1911–1963)

« fly

1   What would happen if you and a group of your classmates were left alone on an island? Would you all work together to survive? Or would you end up killing each other? These are the questions that William Golding asks in his 1954 book *Lord of the Flies*.

2   The story goes like this: A plane crashes on an island somewhere in the Pacific Ocean. The only survivors are a group of young boys. Everything starts

« **plane crash**

out well, but their happiness quickly disappears. Stories of a terrible monster start to drive the boys mad with fear. Soon, they turn from a group of good boys into a pack of wild animals. In fact, the most frightening thing about the book isn't the monster or the wild boys. It's how quickly their little society falls apart.

3 If you ask me, every young person should read this book. It has many important lessons for us all.

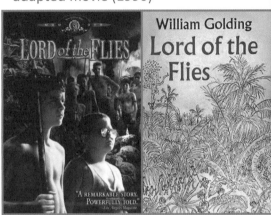

˅ the poster of the adapted movie (1990)

˄ the first UK book cover (1954)

QUESTION

_____ 1. **What is the reading about?**
- a. William Golding.
- b. An island.
- c. A famous book.
- d. A group of boys.

_____ 2. **What are the boys on the island afraid of?**
- a. A ghost.
- b. A monster.
- c. The flies.
- d. Wild animals.

_____ 3. **The writer says that the most frightening thing about the book is how quickly the boys' society falls apart. Is this a fact or an opinion?**
- a. Fact.
- b. Opinion.

_____ 4. **What does the boys' fear make them do?**
- a. Go wild.
- b. Work together.
- c. Leave the island.
- d. Crash their plane.

_____ 5. **What do you think is the writer's opinion of this book?**
- a. He thinks it's boring.
- b. He thinks it's funny.
- c. He thinks it's useless.
- d. He thinks it's excellent.

UNIT
2

Word Study

Synonyms / Antonyms / Words In Context

In this unit, you will practice identifying words with the same or opposite meanings, and guessing the meanings of words from their context. These skills will help you understand new vocabulary and build vocabulary on your own in the future.

21 📺

Why is Sitting Bad for You?

ARE YOU
SITTING TOO MUCH?
SITTING IS KILLING YOU

1   Most people **prefer** sitting to standing. After all, it is much more comfortable! But a new study shows that sitting too much is bad for your health.

2   The study looked at train drivers and train station workers. Both groups ate the same food. The drivers were **overweight** because they sat down all day. But the station workers were not fat because they walked around a lot.

3   Getting fat is only one problem. Sitting too much is bad for your heart. Everyone should move during the day

» exercise

to have a healthy heart. It is bad for your bones, too. They soon become **weak** if you never walk anywhere. **Finally**, sitting is bad for your back. After a while, you will look like a letter "C"!

4   Doctors have some advice for us. They say if you work in an office, stand up every 30 minutes. They also say we shouldn't sit on the sofa all evening. It is better to do some exercise.

≫ weak bones   ≫ slouching

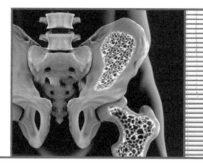

QUESTION

_____ 1. **What does "prefer" mean in the first paragraph?**
   a. Like less.   b. Don't mind.   c. Dislike.   d. Like more.

_____ 2. **What does "overweight" mean in the second paragraph?**
   a. Handsome.   b. Too heavy.   c. Unhappy.   d. Very busy.

_____ 3. **Which word means the opposite of "weak" in the third paragraph?**
   a. Dry.   b. Soft.   c. Poor.   d. Strong.

_____ 4. **Which word means the same as "finally" in the third paragraph?**
   a. Lastly.   b. Clearly.   c. Slowly.   d. Firstly.

_____ 5. **Four people write in their diary for Monday night. Who is NOT following the doctors' advice?**

   a.   b.   c.   d.

Lisa	Arthur	Eric	Amy
Play tennis with Joseph at 19:00	Play video games at 20:15	Go jogging in the park at 18:30	Play basketball at 19:00

22 Team, Let's Join the Fight!

Apple   Yahoo!   Google Maps   YouTube   Wikipedia   News (1002)▾   Popular▾

Fantasy Fight April Competition

1 *Fantasy Fight* is the most exciting online fighting game around! You play as a team of fantasy characters and use magic and skill to beat your **enemies**. Each month we hold a competition to see who has the best *Fantasy Fight* team.

2 Are you part of a *Fantasy Fight* team? Are you better than all the rest? **Sign up** below and get the chance to win a big cash prize!

3 There is a limit of 32 teams for each competition, so **sign up** quickly before places **run out**.

Date & Time:	Saturday, April 9th, 9:00 a.m.
Rules:	1. Each team must have five players.
	2. Each team must be online at least 30 minutes before their first match begins.
	3. Do not be **rude** or mean during the game. Rude players will get a **one-year ban**.
Prizes:	1st place: $200 / 2nd place: $100 / 3rd place: $50

Sign Up ⇒

≽ esports   ≽ keyboard & mouse

QUESTION

_____1. **The phrase** "sign up" **appears several times on the web page.
What is another word for** "sign up"**?**
 a. Fight. b. Leave. c. Join. d. Play.

_____2. "You play as a team of fantasy characters and use magic and skill
to beat your enemies." **What is the opposite of** "enemies"**?**
 a. Fans. b. Friends. c. Players. d. Games.

_____3. "There is a limit of 32 teams for each competition, so sign up quickly
before places run out." **What does it mean if things** "run out"**?**
 a. There are lots of them to choose from.
 b. There are only a few in the world.
 c. There are more and more.
 d. There aren't any left.

_____4. **The rules tell people not to be** "rude." **Which of these is the
opposite of** "rude"**?**
 a. Polite. b. Strong. c. Bright. a. Slow.

_____5. **Breaking one of the rules gets you** "a one-year ban." **What does that
mean?**
 a. You get free things for a year.
 b. You can't join the competition for a year.
 c. You win a one-year-long trip.
 d. You can't play any games for a year.

23

The Voice in My Head

↟ jealous

↟ scream

1
I'm pretty, but not as pretty as you.

I'm smart, but not as smart as you.

I can run fast, but not as fast as you.

I can sing, but not as *sweetly* as you.

2
I wish I had what you have, your *gifts*:

your voice, your brains, your legs, your looks.

It's all I can think of, and it makes me so *bitter*,

how everything I can do, you can do better.

3
There's a voice in my head that says over and over:

I wish you were uglier, stupider, slower,

that every song sounded like *a screaming banshee*.

Then everyone's eyes would finally be on me.

4
But another voice inside me says more softly:

If I keep thinking this way, I will never be happy.

I have to accept it. You are you and I am me.

I won't live my life in jealousy.

QUESTION

_____ 1. **Which of the following words means the same as "sweetly" in the first paragraph?**

   a. Badly.   b. Beautifully.   c. Loudly.   d. Deliciously.

_____ 2. **What does the word "gift" mean in the second paragraph?**

   a. Something special that you were born with.

   b. Something you give to a friend for their birthday.

   c. Something that is cheap and easy to buy.

   d. Something that looks good but isn't real.

_____ 3. **Which of these has the opposite meaning to "bitter" in the second paragraph?**

   a. Sharp.   b. Angry.   c. Happy.   d. Pretty.

_____ 4. **What does the sentence "I won't live my life in jealousy" in the fourth paragraph mean?**

   a. I will try to be kind to people with less money than me.

   b. I will stop trying to get good grades in class.

   c. I will never be friends with a popular person.

   d. I will stop being angry because someone has things I don't.

_____ 5. **In the third paragraph, the writer uses the phrase "a screaming banshee." Which of these is most likely "a screaming banshee"?**

   a.   b.   c.   d.

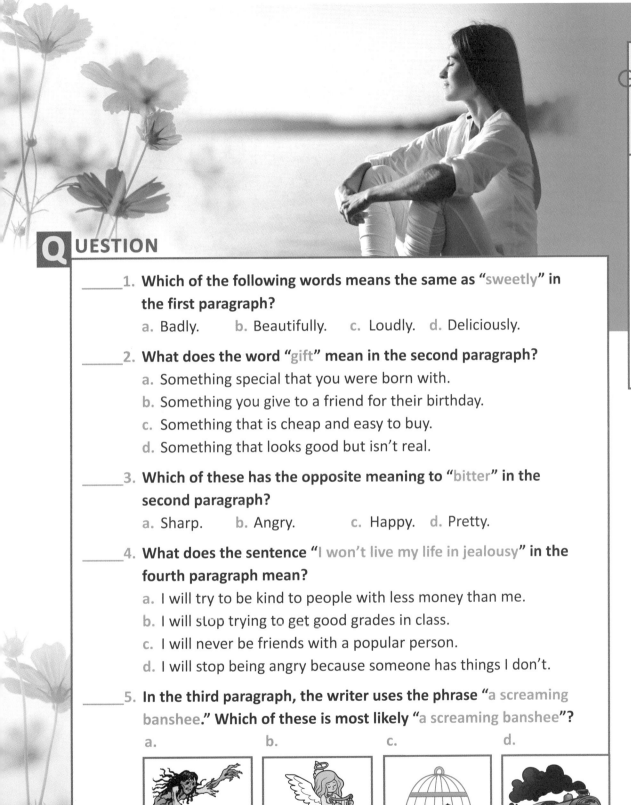

» climate strike

WE'RE SKIPPING LESSONS TO TEACH YOU ONE !

⌃ **Greta Thunberg (2003—)**

Getting the World to Listen

» climate change

1 Greta Thunberg is **no ordinary teenager**. In 2018, at age 15, she began to **skip** school every Friday to go and fight for the planet. Thanks to the Internet, her message spread. Soon more than 20,000 students from around the world were skipping school with her.

2 In 2019, she took a year off school. She wanted to focus on being a leader. That September, she went to a big meeting about climate change in the United States. She **refused** to fly there because she believes that airplanes are bad

» Thunberg speaks before the European Parliament's Environment Committee in 2020.
(cc by European Parliament from EU)

for the environment. So she crossed the ocean by boat. She told world leaders how angry she was with them. She said **they** weren't doing enough to save the planet. Her speech **shocked** a lot of people.

3   Now, everyone knows Greta's message. She is a great example of how young people can get the world to listen.

QUESTION

_____1. **The writer says that Greta Thunberg is "no ordinary teenager." What does this mean?**
    a. She does what people tell her to do.
    b. She wants to see the world.
    c. She is a hard worker and a good student.
    d. She is different from most young people.

_____2. **Which of the following means the same as "skip" in the first paragraph?**
    a. Jump.   b. Miss.   c. Erase.   d. Throw.

_____3. "She refused to fly there because she believes that airplanes are bad for the environment." **Which of the following is the opposite of "refuse"?**
    a. Agree.   b. Begin.   c. Hate.   d. Remember.

_____4. **Who does the word "they" in the second paragraph point to?**
    a. Students.   b. Young people.
    c. World leaders.   d. Airplanes.

_____5. "Her speech shocked a lot of people." **What is another word for "shock"?**
    a. Hurt.   b. Win.   c. Save.   d. Surprise.

Swim, Cycle, Run!

≫ medal

1　Are you good at swimming? How about **cycling** or running? To win a triathlon, you need to be good at all three. A triathlon is one of the hardest sports in the world. First, you do a 1.5 kilometers swim. Next, a 40 kilometers bike ride. And finally, a 10 kilometers run. The fastest person to finish the whole race wins.

2　The first triathlons happened in France in the 1920s. But triathlons did not become popular until very recently. These days, **in the United States alone**, around 500,000 people do triathlons each year.

3　There are many different **versions** of triathlons. Some examples are the mini-triathlon and the winter triathlon. But the most famous (and **toughest**) is the Ironman triathlon. An Ironman triathlon is more than twice as long as a regular **one**. Only the best finish an Ironman race. Could you be one of them?

≪ the winners of 2014 Garmin Barcelona Triathlon in the women's category

⌃ The fastest person wins.

QUESTION

_____1. **What does the word "cycling" mean in the first paragraph?**
  a. Driving a car.   b. Climbing a mountain.
  c. Jumping out of a plane.   d. Riding a bicycle.

_____2. **"These days, in the United States alone, around 500,000 people do triathlons each year." What does the phrase "in the United States alone" mean?**
  a. Outside the United States.   b. Just in the United States.
  c. Not in the United States.   d. Near the United States.

_____3. **Which of the following has the same meaning as "versions" in the third paragraph?**
  a. Types.   b. Fans.   c. Rules.   d. Places.

_____4. **Which of the following is the opposite of "toughest" in the third paragraph?**
  a. Hardest.   b. Most popular.
  c. Easiest.   d. Most expensive.

_____5. **What does the word "one" point to in the third paragraph?**
  a. Person.   b. Triathlon.   c. Year.   d. Country.

» athlete

26 Ouch! My Tooth Hurts!

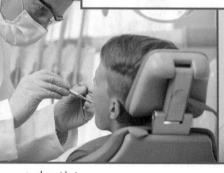
≪ dentist

≪ brushing one's teeth

≪ mouthwash

date: **March 23rd, Friday**

Dear Diary,

1   This morning my tooth started to hurt really badly. I was in so much pain. I couldn't eat anything. At lunch, I could only drink warm water.

2   After school, Mom said we should go to see the dentist. I didn't want to go. I'm **frightened** of dentists. But the pain was so bad! So **in the end**, I agreed. The dentist looked at my tooth and gave me something to stop the pain. Then he started to work. **Fortunately** this dentist was very good at his job. It was **over** very quickly.

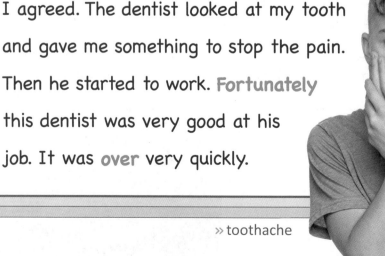

≫ toothache

3   Before I left, the dentist asked me if I ate a lot of candy or drink a lot of soda. I said yes, I did. He told me I should stop that if I wanted healthy teeth. And he said I should brush my teeth after every meal.

4   From now on, Diary, I promise to keep my teeth super clean!

» soda

Q UESTION

_____ 1. **What is another word for** "frightened" **in the second paragraph?**
    a. Scared.   b. Bored.   c. Tired.   d. Shy.

_____ 2. **What does the phrase** "in the end" **mean in the second paragraph?**
    a. Without waiting.   b. After a while.
    c. Never.   d. A long time ago.

_____ 3. **What is another word for** "fortunately" **in the sentence** "Fortunately, this dentist was good at his job"?
    a. Slowly.   b. Badly.   c. Luckily.   d. Stupidly.

_____ 4. **What is another word for** "over" **in the sentence** "It was over very quickly"?
    a. Finished.   b. Painful.   c. Expensive.   d. Broken.

_____ 5. **What does the word** "that" **point to in the sentence** "He told me I should stop that if I wanted healthy teeth"?
    a. Brushing my teeth after every meal.
    b. Being frightened of the dentist.
    c. Drinking warm water.
    d. Eating candy and drinking soda.

» pink Himalayan salt

Too Much of a Good Thing

A little bit of salt makes your food taste great. But did you know that too much is bad for your **brain**? [1]

Scientists in New York fed mice very salty meals for many weeks. After just eight weeks, the mice began acting strangely. They forgot things. They couldn't build **nests**. And they couldn't find their way through simple mazes. Mice should be able to do these things with no **difficulty**. In people, this would mean you couldn't put on clothes, find your classroom, or do other simple things. [2]

⌃ a mouse in a maze

So how much salt would you need to eat before you started to feel strange? Luckily, it is quite a lot—around five to six times the normal amount. Of course, these days, there is salt in **just about** everything. And often you are eating more than you know. But don't worry. If you do your best to eat healthily, the amount of salt you take in should be **harmless**.

QUESTION

_____1. **The writer says that salt is "bad for your brain." Which of the following is a picture of a "brain"?**

a. 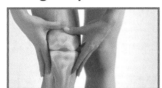   b.

c. 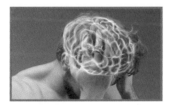   d.

_____2. **Mice "couldn't build nests" after they ate too much salt. What is a "nest"?**
a. A place to live.   b. A kind of food.
c. A type of game.   d. A maze.

_____3. **"Mice should be able to do these things with no difficulty." What is another word for "difficulty"?**
a. Breakfast   b. Clothes.   c. Money.   d. Problem.

_____4. **"Of course, these days, there is salt in just about everything!" What is another word for "just about"?**
a. Pretty.   b. Almost.   c. Totally.   d. Enough.

_____5. **Which of these is the opposite of "harmless" in the final sentence?**
a. Delicious.   b. Heavy.   c. Small.   d. Dangerous.

» thief

Keep Your Eyes Open! 👁 👁

Warning!
Thief in the Area!

1   Yesterday evening someone stole a bicycle from the neighborhood. The bike belonged to Mr. James White at 21 Wood Street and it was in his garden. A neighbor **witnessed** a man walking down the street with Mr. White's bicycle at 7 p.m. The man was tall, with long brown hair and a long beard. He was wearing a black jacket and a dark blue baseball hat. If you see this man, please tell the neighborhood police **immediately**.

2   Also, please don't leave anything **valuable** outside. Keep any bicycles inside. And remember to keep your cars and all doors and windows locked **at all times**. We will do our best to keep everyone and their things safe. But we ask you all to **keep your eyes open**! Help us catch this thief!

Thank you,

The Neighborhood Police

⌃ long beard

⌃ neighborhood

⌃ bicycle

QUESTION

_____ 1. "A neighbor witnessed a man walking down the street with Mr. White's bicycle at 7 p.m." **What does "witness" mean?**

a. See. b. Draw. c. Forget. d. Hear.

_____ 2. **The police say you should tell them immediately if you see the thief. What is the opposite of "immediately"?**

a. Truly. b. Quickly. c. Well. d. Later.

_____ 3. **The police ask people not to leave anything valuable outside. Which of these is another word for "valuable"?**

a. Cheap. b. Colorful. c. Expensive. d. Dark.

_____ 4. "And remember to keep your cars and all doors and windows locked at all times." **What does the phrase "at all times" mean?**

a. Always. b. Never. c. Sometimes. d. On weekends.

_____ 5. "But we ask you all to keep your eyes open!" **What does the phrase "keep your eyes open" mean?**

a. Take a break. b. Watch carefully.

c. Do not fall asleep. d. Take a photo.

⌃ ice sheet

Sailing Stones

1   Can a **heavy** stone move by itself, without help from a person? The answer is yes! It looks like magic, but it isn't. And it only happens on the floor of a playa.

2   A playa is an area of dry, flat land. When it rains, water goes into the playa floor. At night, it gets cold. The top of the water becomes a **thin** sheet of ice. The ice sheet rests above the water. In the morning, the sun comes out. The ice **begins** to break. When it breaks, it pushes the stones on the playa floor. They can move five meters in one minute! That means their **speed** is 0.3 kilometers an hour.

⌄ moving stones on the playa floor

« Death Valley National Park

« sunrise

3 For many years, nobody knew how the stones moved. But in 2014 some people studied the stones carefully. They did their study in Death Valley National Park, California. They used GPS and made a long video of the stones.

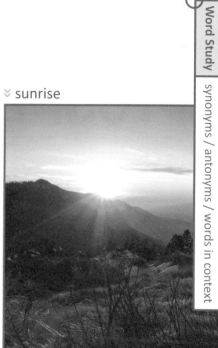

QUESTION

_____ 1. **Which word is the opposite of "heavy" in the first paragraph?**
   a. Square.   b. Happy.   c. Light.   d. Glass.

_____ 2. **Which word is the opposite of "thin" in the second paragraph?**
   a. Soft.   b. Thick.   c. Green.   d. Warm.

_____ 3. **Which word means the same as "begins" in the second paragraph?**
   a. Walks.   b. Starts.   c. Calls.   d. Turns.

_____ 4. **What does "speed" mean in the second paragraph?**
   a. How fast something goes.
   b. How tall something is.
   c. How much something costs.
   d. How old something is.

_____ 5. **What does "carefully" mean in the third paragraph?**
   a. Taking a break because you worked hard on something.
   b. Doing something in a way so that you don't make a mistake.
   c. Getting angry because something is not working.
   d. Showing that you don't understand something well.

30 Celebrate Your Family!

⌄ father and daughter

⌃ grandparent family

1   When you think of a family, what do you **picture** in your mind? Is it a mom, dad, and children? Many people have this idea of a family. But there are lots of one-parent families **out there** too.

2   Some think that one-parent families are "broken." As a result, children from **this kind of family** often feel bad. But are one-parent families really worse than two-parent families?

3   Ask yourself—**when it comes to** family, what is really important? Do the children feel loved? Do they have plenty of food to eat? Are they healthy and safe? If the answer to these questions is yes, does it really matter if there is only one parent? Of course not!

4   So if you are from a one-parent family, don't be **ashamed**. What's important isn't the number of parents you have. It is what kind of parent you have. If you have a great mom or dad, don't be afraid to celebrate it!

≫ mother and son

≫ nuclear family

QUESTION

_____ 1. **What is another word for "picture" in the first paragraph?**

a. Jump.　　b. See.　　c. Lose.　　d. Take.

_____ 2. **What does the phrase "out there" mean in the first paragraph?**

a. In the world.　　　b. In the sea.

c. In space.　　　　d. In school.

_____ 3. **What does "this kind of family" mean in the second paragraph?**

a. One-parent families.　　b. Two-parent families.

c. Families with one child.　　d. Families with two children.

_____ 4. **"Ask yourself—when it comes to family, what is really important?" What does the phrase "when it comes to (something)" mean?**

a. When you choose something.

b. When you hate something.

c. When you want to make something.

d. When you think about something.

_____ 5. **"So if you are from a one-parent family, don't be ashamed." Which of these is the opposite of "ashamed"?**

a. Proud.　　b. Loud.　　c. Happy.　　d. Lazy.

UNIT
3

Study Strategies

3-1
Visual Materials

3-2
Reference Sources

Visual material like charts and graphs, and reference sources like indexes and dictionaries, all provide important information. What's more, they help you understand complicated information more quickly than you can by reading. In this unit, you will learn to use them to gather information.

31 What Your Body Needs

1 Your body needs several things to work well. It needs energy to keep it moving. (We measure energy in calories). It also needs protein. Protein helps you grow. It also helps your body fix itself when it is broken. Your body can store energy as fat, but it cannot store protein. So it is important to eat enough protein each day.

2 Each day, people need around 0.8 grams of protein per kilogram of body weight. For example, if you weigh 65 kilograms, you need 52 grams of protein (0.8 x 65). Some foods have lots of protein. Others much less. The table on the next page shows you how many grams of protein each food has per 150 calories.

3 A table arranges information in columns (down) and rows (across). To find out how much protein each food has, first find it in the left column. Then look across to the protein column.

Grams of Protein per 150 Calories

	Food	Protein
	Pork	23 g
	Sushi	12 g
	Steak	23 g
	Cheese	16 g
	Milk	10 g

	Food	Protein
	Egg White	24 g
	Tomato	1 g
	Shrimp	11 g
	Donut	4 g
	Oatmeal	4 g

QUESTION

_____1. **Which type of food has the most amount of protein?**

    a. Pork.   **b.** Shrimp.   **c.** Egg white.   **d.** Pepper.

_____2. **Which of the following is TRUE?**

    a. Milk has more protein than sushi.

    b. Pork and steak have the same amount of protein.

    c. Oatmeal has more protein than cheese.

    d. Tomato and pork have the same amount of protein.

_____3. **Which of the following is NOT true?**

    a. Cheese has more protein than sushi.

    b. Oatmeal has more protein than tomato.

    c. Tomato has more protein than pork.

    d. Donut has more protein than tomato.

_____4. **My doctor told me to eat more protein. Which of these foods should I eat more of?**

    a. Cheese.   **b.** Tomato.   **c.** Oatmeal.   **d.** Pork.

_____5. **Which food has more protein than milk, but less protein than sushi?**

    a. Shrimp.   **b.** Oatmeal.   **c.** Steak.   **d.** Cheese.

UNIT 3 🎧 32

32

No Internet at Home? No Problem!

1   We do almost everything online these days. We get our news online. We find places to eat online. And we talk with our friends online. Having the Internet is now a human right.

⌃ video chat

However, more and more people do not have home Internet. Instead, they use their phones to go online.

2   As a result, people are getting used to using the Internet "on-the-go." This makes people more and more reliant on their phones. We know this is bad for people's health. Many now can't be without their phones for even a few minutes.

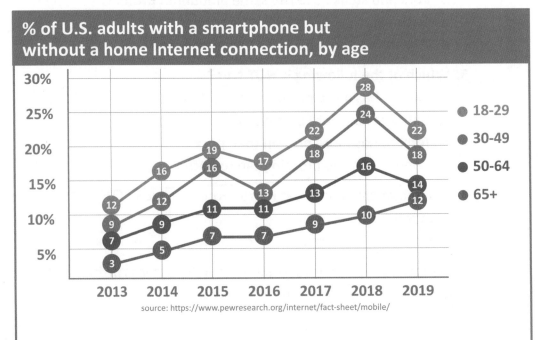

% of U.S. adults with a smartphone but without a home Internet connection, by age

- 18-29
- 30-49
- 50-64
- 65+

source: https://www.pewresearch.org/internet/fact-sheet/mobile/

3   The line graph on the previous page shows the percentage (%) of adults in the United States with a smartphone but with no home Internet. A line graph shows numbers as points. A line then joins these points together. This way it is easy to see how numbers change over time.

≫ phone addiction

≪ phubber

QUESTION

_____1. **What percentage of 18–29-year-olds had a smartphone but no home Internet in 2015?**
   a. 19%   b. 5%   c. 11%   d. 28%

_____2. **Sixteen percent of which age group had a smartphone but no home Internet in 2018?**
   a. 18–29   b. 30–49   c. 50–64   d. 65+

_____3. **In which year did 5% of people aged 65 and over have a smartphone but no home Internet?**
   a. 2013   b. 2014   c. 2017   d. 2019

_____4. **Which of the following is TRUE?**
   a. The numbers went up for 30–49-year-olds between 2015 and 2016.
   b. The numbers went up for 50–64-year-olds between 2018 and 2019.
   c. The numbers went down for 18–29-year-olds between 2013 and 2014.
   d. The numbers for 50–64-year-olds stayed the same between 2015 and 2016.

_____5. **Which of the following is NOT true?**
   a. Between 2013 and 2019, the numbers for the oldest age group never dropped.
   b. The numbers for 30–49-year-olds were higher in 2015 than in 2016.
   c. The numbers for 18–29-year-olds were lower in 2019 than in 2016.
   d. The numbers for the youngest age group were always the highest each year.

33 🐾 New House, New Pet

1 My family doesn't have a pet. We live in a small apartment in the city, and my parents said we don't have enough room. Next month we are moving to a bigger house in the countryside.

⌃ apartment

I was mad at first, but then my parents said we could have a pet! They even said I could decide which animal to have. I was so happy. But I'm finding it hard to choose between a dog and a cat.

Dog

- Listens to you
- Can be very big
- Always happy to see you
- Needs lots of attention
- Can teach it tricks
- Have to walk it every day
- Shows you a lot of love
- Noisy
- Goes to the bathroom outside

(Both)
- •• Have to feed it
- •• Might break furniture
- •• Can live outside or inside
- •• Can pet it
- •• Gets hair everywhere

Cat

- Might ignore you
- Does whatever it wants
- Won't dig up the garden
- Cleans itself
- Sleeps a lot
- Does funny, cute things
- Can leave it alone for a few days
- Goes to the bathroom in a box
- Don't have to take it for a walk

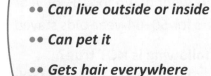

⌃ countryside

2 To make things clearer in my mind, I drew a Venn diagram. A Venn diagram has two circles. In my diagram, one circle has information just about cats. And the other one has information just about dogs. In the middle, the two circles overlap. This is where I put information about both dogs and cats. Now I can see clearly what is different and similar about these two pets!

QUESTION

_____1. **Which of these is ONLY true about a cat?**
   a. It cleans itself.   b. You have to walk it every day.
   c. You have to feed it.   d. It gets hair everywhere.

_____2. **Which of these is NOT true about a dog?**
   a. It is always happy to see you.   b. It can live inside or outside.
   c. It can learn new tricks.   d. It sleeps a lot.

_____3. **Which of these is true about BOTH a cat and a dog?**
   a. It is always happy to see you.   b. It gets hair everywhere.
   c. It goes to the bathroom in a box.   d. It is noisy.

_____4. **Which of these is NOT true about a cat?**
   a. You can leave it alone for a few days. b. It does whatever it wants.
   c. It might ignore you.   d. It shows you a lot of love.

_____5. **If the writer really wants a pet and also wants to grow flowers and vegetables in the garden of her new house, which animal do you think she will choose?**
   a. A dog.   b. A cat.
   c. A dog and a cat.   d. Not a dog or a cat.

04 A Much-Needed Change

≪ metal straw

≫ plastic pollution

REDUCE

REUSE

RECYCLE

1   We all love a cold drink on a warm day. In the past, we would use a plastic straw to drink it. But times are changing. Many countries are now banning plastic straws. If you want to use a straw to drink your juice or milk tea, you now have to use a metal or paper one.

2   Why are countries making this change? Because plastic straws do not disappear over time. They get into the rivers and the seas and hurt the animals there. They also break down into smaller pieces and pollute the water and the earth.

3   But did we really use to throw away that many straws? Yes! Look at the bar graph on the next page. It shows the number of straws people threw away in 2018 in nine European countries alone. A bar graph shows numbers as bars of different sizes. This makes it easy to compare different numbers.

Number of Plastic Straws Used in 2018 (in billions*)

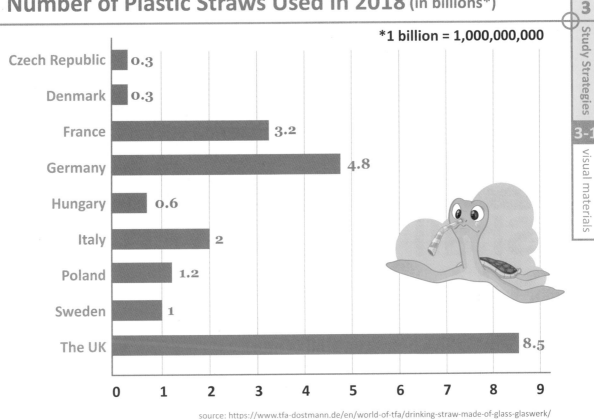

*1 billion = 1,000,000,000

Czech Republic	0.3
Denmark	0.3
France	3.2
Germany	4.8
Hungary	0.6
Italy	2
Poland	1.2
Sweden	1
The UK	8.5

source: https://www.tfa-dostmann.de/en/world-of-tfa/drinking-straw-made-of-glass-glaswerk/

QUESTION

_____ 1. **Which country used the most plastic straws in 2018?**
   a. The UK.   b. Sweden.   c. Italy.   d. Hungary.

_____ 2. **How many straws did France use in 2018?**
   a. 1.2 billion.   b. 0.6 billion.   c. 3.2 billion.   d. 4.8 billion.

_____ 3. **Which countries used the fewest plastic straws in 2018?**
   a. Denmark and Hungary.   b. Denmark and the Czech Republic.
   c. Denmark and France.   d. Denmark and Germany.

_____ 4. **Which of the following is TRUE?**
   a. Sweden used fewer plastic straws than Hungary.
   b. Hungary used fewer plastic straws than Denmark.
   c. Poland used fewer plastic straws than Sweden.
   d. Germany used more plastic straws than Poland.

_____ 5. **Which country used 2 billion plastic straws in 2018?**
   a. Germany.   b. Italy.   c. France.   d. The UK.

≫ mystery movie ≫ horror movie

∧ animation movie

Shall We Watch a Movie?

1 What's your favorite kind of movie? Do you like action movies, with fighting and guns? Or do you like comedies—funny movies with lots of jokes? How about dramas—serious stories about difficult lives? Maybe you like romances—movies with a nice love story. Or perhaps you prefer science fiction (or "sci-fi") movies, with UFOs and time-travel.

2 Everyone has their own favorite. But some movies are more popular with boys and others with girls. That's why, if you have a mixed group of friends, it can be hard to agree on what movie to watch!

3 In my school, we asked 100 boys and 100 girls to name their favorite kind of movie. The results are the two pie charts on the next page. A pie chart shows numbers as pieces of a circle. The bigger the piece of pie, the higher the number. This way, you can easily see which number has the biggest or smallest share of the total.

^ movie actress and actor

■ comedy

■ action

■ romance

■ drama

■ sci-fi

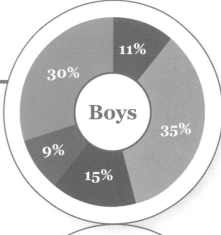

Boys

11%

30%

35%

9%

15%

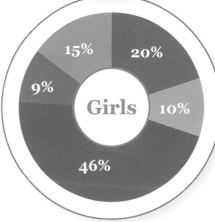

Girls

15%

20%

9%

10%

46%

Q UESTION

_____ 1. **Which of these movie types did boys like more than girls?**
   a. Romance. **b.** Drama. **c.** Sci-fi. **d.** Comedy.

_____ 2. **Which of these movie types was the most popular with girls?**
   a. Drama. **b.** Comedy. **c.** Action. **d.** Romance.

_____ 3. **What percentage of boys said romance was their favorite movie type?**
   a. 15% **b.** 46% **c.** 9% **d.** 11%

_____ 4. **Which of the following is NOT true?**
   a. Eleven percent of boys said comedy was their favorite movie type.
   b. Ten percent of girls said action was their favorite movie type.
   c. Fifteen percent of girls said sci-fi was their favorite movie type.
   d. Twenty percent of boys said drama was their favorite movie type.

_____ 5. **Which of the following is TRUE?**
   a. More boys chose drama as their favorite movie type than girls.
   b. The favorite movie type among boys was sci-fi.
   c. Drama was the least favorite movie type for both boys and girls.
   d. The least favorite movie type among girls was action.

36

Say It Out Loud!

1 Many people are scared of public speaking. Just thinking about it makes them nervous. However, most of us will have to do it at some point in our lives.

⌃ nervous

2 One of the biggest mistakes many speakers make is learning their lines. They spend hours trying to remember each word of their speech. But this is actually one of the worst things you can do. A better way is to just remember your key points. This allows you to speak more naturally and even change your speech quickly if you need to.

3 For more advice about public speaking, why not buy a book about it? A good book will teach you all kinds of useful tips and tricks. On the next page is the table of contents for the book *Level Up Your Public Speaking*. The table of contents shows you the names/topics of each chapter along with what page to turn to.

» lectern

Contents

QUESTION

_____1. **What page does the chapter "How Loud?" start on?**
   a. 10   **b.** 70   **c.** 38   **d.** 22

_____2. **What chapter should you read if you want to learn the best way to prepare your speech?**
   a. Chapter 1.   **b.** Chapter 3.   **c.** Chapter 6.   **d.** Chapter 7.

_____3. **What is Part Two of the book called?**
   a. Get Confident.   **b.** The Basics.
   c. Why Are You Afraid?   **d.** Where to Look.

_____4. **What is the chapter just before "Get Excited About Your Subject"?**
   a. Think About Succeeding.   **b.** How to Stand.
   c. How Loud?   **d.** How to Prepare Well.

_____5. **Where would you find the advice the writer told you in the second paragraph of the reading?**
   a. Chapter 2.   **b.** Chapter 4.   **c.** Chapter 5.   **d.** Chapter 9.

« Hippos have large teeth.

˅ Hippos look funny with their big, round bodies.

Funny-Looking, but Dangerous!

1   Hippos are large African mammals. They live in rivers and look quite funny with their little ears and big, round, gray bodies. But in fact, they are one of the world's most dangerous animals. Hippos get angry very easily. They have large teeth. And they can run really fast. Every year, they kill around 500 people in Africa.

2   Some people also say hippos sweat blood! Scary, right? Yes, if it were true. A hippo's sweat is red, but it isn't blood. It is actually a type of oil. This special oil protects a hippo's skin from the hot African sun.

3   I first saw the word hippo in a book about Africa. I had to look it up in a dictionary because I didn't know what it meant. I found the word on a page in the H section. Take a look at some of the other words on that page. They all start with the letters "hi–."

hippie

hippie /ˈhɪpi/ noun [C] someone in the 1960s who was opposed to war and the traditional attitudes of society, and who showed this by having long hair and wearing very informal clothes

hippo /ˈhɪpəʊ/ noun [C] *informal* a HIPPOPOTAMUS

hip ˈpocket noun [C] a pocket near your HIP in a pair of trousers or a skirt

the Hippocratic oath /ˌhɪpəˌkrætɪk ˈəʊθ/ noun the promise that doctors make to respect the moral principles of the medical profession

hippopotamus /ˌhɪpəˈpɒtəməs/ noun [C] a large African animal with a wide head and mouth and thick grey skin. Hippopotamuses live in or near rivers. —*picture* → C12

hippy /ˈhɪpi/ another spelling of **hippie**

hipsters /ˈhɪpstə(r)z/ noun [plural] *British* trousers that fit tightly around your HIPS and do not cover your waist

hire¹ /ˈhaɪə(r)/ verb ★★
1 [T] *British* if you hire something, such as a car, room, or piece of equipment, you pay the owner so that you can use it, especially for a short time. The usual American word is **rent**: *You can hire a car at the airport.*
2 [I/T] to pay someone to work for you, especially for a short time = EMPLOY: *I hired someone to paint the house.*
♦ **hire and fire** *His main responsibility is hiring and firing.*
3 hire or **hire out** [T] *British spoken* to let someone use something temporarily in return for money. The usual American word for this is **rent out**: *There are several companies that hire office equipment to businesses.*
　PHRASAL VERB ˌhire ˈout [T] **1** *British same as* **hire¹** 3: *This room is often hired out for private parties.* **2** to send someone to work for other people for short periods of time in return for payment: **hire yourself out** *He earned his living by hiring himself out to whoever needed his services.*

hire² /ˈhaɪə(r)/ noun [U] *British* ★ the payment of money in order to use something, especially for a short time. The usual American word is **rental**: *It's cheaper to pay for your car hire before you go.* ♦ *We paid £50 for the hire of the hall.* **a.** [only before noun] used for describing a vehicle that has been hired or a company from which you can hire a vehicle or equipment. The usual American word is **rental**: *a hire car/van* ♦ *a tool hire company*
　PHRASES **for hire 1** available to be hired: *There were motorcycles for hire.* **2** available to be employed in a particular job: *The agency helps people find childcare, including putting families in touch with nannies for hire.*
on hire *British* used for saying that something is being hired: *All their cars were already out on hire.*

hired gun /ˌhaɪə(r)d ˈɡʌn/ noun [C] **1** someone who is paid to kill someone = HITMAN **2** an expert who is employed to solve a problem

hired hand /ˌhaɪə(r)d ˈhænd/ noun [C] someone who is hired to work on a farm, especially for a short period of time

hireling /ˈhaɪə(r)lɪŋ/ noun [C] *mainly literary* someone who is willing to do unpleasant or illegal jobs for people in order to earn money

hire ˈpurchase noun [U] *British* a method of buying expensive goods in which you pay small regular amounts of money until you have paid the whole amount. The American word is **installment plan**.

hirsute /ˈhɜː(r)ˌsjuːt/ adj *mainly literary* a hirsute man has a lot of hair on his face or body = HAIRY

(source: Macmillan English Dictionary for Advanced Learner [New Edition])

pink sweat

QUESTION

_____1. **What is true about the word "hippo"?**
　a. It is a verb.
　b. It comes after "hire."
　c. It is short for "hippopotamus."
　d. It comes before "hippie."

_____2. **What kind of word is "hip pocket"?**
　a. An adjective.　　b. An adverb.
　c. A noun.　　　　d. A verb.

_____3. **What does the word "hirsute" mean?**
　a. Old and important.
　b. Hairy.
　c. The past.
　d. The sound a snake makes.

_____4. **Which of the following words comes after "hired gun"?**
　a. Hip pocket.　　b. Hipsters.
　c. Hire.　　　　　d. Hired hand.

_____5. **What is TRUE about the word "hippy"?**
　a. It is an adjective.
　b. It is another way to spell "hippie."
　c. It is a type of chart.
　d. It comes after "historically."

38

Taiwan's First People

1   Taiwan is home to over 23 million people. A little over 2% (around 560,000) are Taiwanese aborigines. Taiwanese aborigines came to Taiwan thousands of years ago. They used to live all over Taiwan. But in the 1600s,

⌃ Amis' harvest festival

people from China and Europe began coming to the island. They fought with the aborigines for control of the land. Now, Taiwanese aborigines mostly live on the island's east coast and in the central mountains.

2   There are 16 different groups of Taiwanese aborigines. They all have their own customs, festivals, and language. The largest of these 16 groups is the Amis, with a little over 200,000 people. From the map, you can see the Amis live in the central part of Taiwan's east coast. The map also has information about other groups. By looking at the map, you can see where Taiwan's aboriginal groups live.

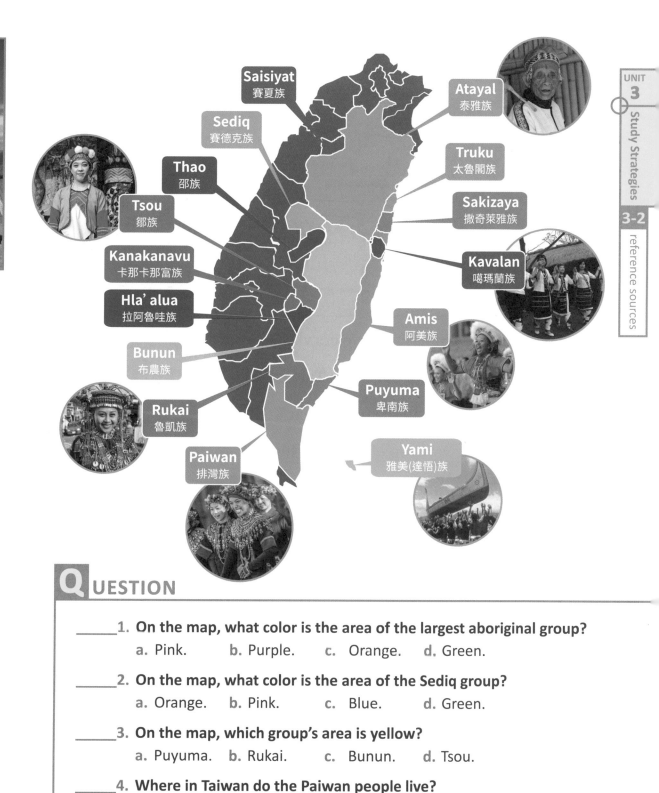

QUESTION

_____1. **On the map, what color is the area of the largest aboriginal group?**
   a. Pink.　　**b.** Purple.　　**c.** Orange.　　**d.** Green.

_____2. **On the map, what color is the area of the Sediq group?**
   a. Orange.　**b.** Pink.　　**c.** Blue.　　**d.** Green.

_____3. **On the map, which group's area is yellow?**
   a. Puyuma.　**b.** Rukai.　　**c.** Bunun.　　**d.** Tsou.

_____4. **Where in Taiwan do the Paiwan people live?**
   a. In the south-east.　　**b.** In the north-west.
   c. In the north-east.　　**d.** In the center.

_____5. **Which group's land does NOT touch any other group's land?**
   a. Saisiyat.　**b.** Amis.　　**c.** Bunun.　　**d.** Yami.

39

A Great Place to Travel

≪ surfing

≪ Mass Rapid Transit (MRT)

≪ Sun Moon Lake

1 More and more foreign travelers visit Taiwan each year. They shop for snacks in Taiwan's big cities. They go surfing in the ocean near Kenting. They climb to the very top of Taiwan's highest mountains. But most importantly, they all have a great time!

2 Getting around Taiwan as a tourist is easy. In Taipei, you can get from place to place in no time on the MRT! If you want to get away from the city, beautiful spots like Sun Moon Lake are just a short bus or train ride away.

3 Travelers in Taiwan often have a guidebook with them. In the back of the book, there is an index. This is a list of everything in the guidebook and the pages you need to turn to. An index lists things in alphabetical order—that is, from A to Z. Here is a small section of the index from a guidebook about Taiwan.

Index

QUESTION

_____1. **On what pages would you find information about Sun Moon Lake?**

  a. 64-5   **b.** 181-8

  c. 135-6   **d.** 218-21

_____2. **What would you find information about on pages 144-5?**

  a. Snow Mountain.

  b. Sileng Hot Spring.

  c. Snake Alley.

  d. Su Ho Paper Museum.

_____3. **You want to find out about the weather in southern Taiwan. What page should you turn to?**

  a. 230   **b.** 37

  c. 271   **d.** 236

_____4. **The index does not have an entry for the little village of Smangus. If it did, where would the entry be?**

  a. Between "stinky tofu" and "Su Ho Paper Museum."

  b. Between "Shuili" and "Shuitou."

  c. Between "Sixty Stone Mountain" and "Snake Alley."

  d. Between "shopping" and "shrimp fishing."

_____5. **How many pages are there in the book about Taiwan's snakes?**

  a. One.   **b.** Two.

  c. Five.   **d.** Eight.

UNIT
3

Study Strategies

3-2

reference sources

40

A Delicious New Dish

1 Today I went to my friend Raya's house to study. Raya's mom asked me if I wanted to stay for dinner. Raya's mom is from Indonesia. I really wanted to try some Indonesian food. So I said, "Yes, please!" We ate *nasi goreng*—Indonesian-style fried rice. It is similar to Taiwanese fried rice. But it has a lot more flavor. It comes with a fried egg on top! It was so delicious. I asked Raya's mom for the recipe. Here is what she wrote down for me:

» garlic

» small onion

» cucumber

Nasi Goreng

serving: 4 people

Ingredients

- chicken (50 g)
- kecap manis
  (sweet soy sauce) (3 tablespoons)
- garlic (2 pieces)
- 1 red chili
- 1 small onion
- cooked white rice (750 g)
- shrimp paste (2 teaspoons)
- 4 eggs
- 2 tomatoes
- 1 cucumber
- 1 lime   » shrimp paste

(cc by D.W. Fisher-Freberg)

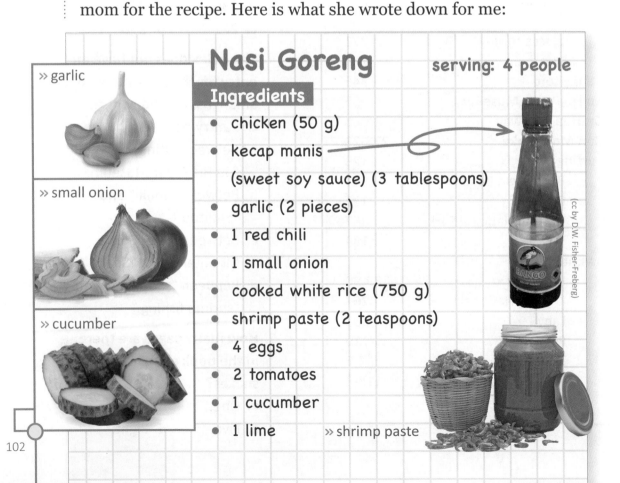

Directions

1. Cut up the chili and garlic. Add to a hot pan.
2. Cut up the onion. Add to the pan.
3. Cut up the chicken into small pieces. Add to the pan. Cook until it turns white.
4. Add the rice, kecap manis, and the shrimp paste. Cook for 2 minutes.
5. Cut up the tomatoes, cucumber, and lime.
6. Fry the eggs.
7. Serve the rice with a fried egg on top and some tomatoes, cucumber, and lime on the side.

QUESTION

_____1. **How many tomatoes does Raya's mom use in her *nasi goreng*?**
   a. Four.   b. Two.   c. One.   d. Three.

_____2. **What is the first step in making *nasi goreng*?**
   a. Cook the onion.
   b. Add the *kecap manis* to the pan.
   c. Cut up the chili and garlic.
   d. Cut up the cucumber.

_____3. **Which of these ingredients is NOT in *nasi goreng*?**
   a. Eggs.   b. Rice.   c. Chicken.   d. Banana.

_____4. **Which of the following is TRUE about making *nasi goreng*?**
   a. You do not need to cook the tomatoes.
   b. You need to use one big onion.
   c. The onion is the last thing to go into the pan.
   d. You need to use five tablespoons of *kecap manis*.

_____5. **If you have eight people coming for dinner, how many eggs will you need?**
   a. Four.   b. Five.   c. Eight.   d. Two.

UNIT
4

Final Review

Choosing the Right Path

🔒 https://www.yourfuture.com/jobs/important-advice

Choosing Your Future Job — Some Important Advice

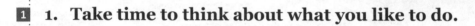

1. Take time to think about what you like to do.

You will probably spend many hours of your day at your job. So it's best if you enjoy it! Take some time to think about what you really enjoy doing and why.

2. Learn about the different kinds of jobs.

There are so many different types of jobs out there. Learn about them! That way, you are more likely to find the one for you.

3. Remember to follow your own path.

Don't worry about what other people in your school want to do. Everyone is different. It is your future, not theirs!

4. Try it out.

If you want to be a writer, start writing for your school newspaper. If you want to be a soccer coach, ask if you can help coach your school team. See for yourself if that job is right for you.

QUESTION

_____1. **What is the reading about?**
    a. How to pick a future job.   **b.** How to get a job at a newspaper.
    c. What jobs will be like in the future.   **d.** Which jobs make the most money.

_____2. **Which of the following is NOT the writer's advice.**
    a. Think about what you like to do.
    b. Learn about the different kinds of jobs.
    c. Choose the same job as everyone else in your class.
    d. Try the job and see if you like it.

_____3. **"You will probably spend many hours of your day at your job. So it's best if you enjoy it!" Is this a fact or the writer's opinion?**
    a. Fact.   **b.** Opinion.

_____4. **Why should you learn about the different kinds of jobs?**
    a. You will learn how to be make your future boss happy.
    b. You will have a bigger chance of finding a job you like.
    c. You will be able to get any job you want.
    d. You will get all the skills you need to do your future job well.

_____5. **You are reading this page of the Your Future website.
What would be a good title for this page?**

● ● ● ← | →   🔒 https://www.yourfuture.com/jobs

Click on the pictures to find out why these people like their jobs.

Joe Jones	_Mary Hills_	_Ben Green_	_Jane Saunders_	_Martin Rees_
Teacher	Police Officer	Cook	Doctor	Farmer

    a. Study Plan   **b.** The World's Hardest Jobs
    c. A Farmer's Life   **d.** Hear From Real People

42 Watch of the Future

1   Gadgets are everywhere now. There are watches, phones, and health gadgets, and all of them are smart. But that's a lot of things you need to buy. Wouldn't it be nice if just one gadget could do it all?

2   Well luckily there is one!

3   I'm talking about the FitPro—the only gadget you will ever need. Want to send a text to a friend? It can do that. Want to check your heart health? It can do that too. In fact, the FitPro can do just about everything, including:

🎵 play music   👣 count your steps each day

📍 show where you are on a map

📷 take pictures   📞 make phone calls

4   FitPro isn't just useful; **it also looks great!** It comes in three different colors: red, blue, and black. Some of the biggest names in the watch world helped design it.

5   **Don't wait! Order today and get $150 off your FitPro. Order at: <u>www.fitpro.com</u>.**

⌃ sending a text

⌃ gadget

QUESTION

_____1. **What is the third paragraph about?**

    a. Where you can find the FitPro.

    b. How much the FitPro costs.

    c. What the FitPro looks like.

    d. What the FitPro can do.

_____2. **What is the main idea of the first paragraph?**

    a. There are too many different gadgets.

    b. Gadgets are important.

    c. The FitPro is a gadget.

    d. Gadgets are not expensive.

_____3. **Is "it also looks great" from the reading a fact or the writer's opinion?**

    a. Fact.   **b.** Opinion.

_____4. **Which of the following is NOT something that the FitPro can do?**

    a. Take pictures.   **b.** Make phone calls.

    c. Check heart health.   **d.** Play movies.

_____5. **Which of the following is probably TRUE?**

    a. The price of the FitPro is over $150.

    b. The FitPro is hard to find.

    c. The FitPro is very heavy.

    d. There are more than three colors of FitPro.

43 A Summer to Remember

≫ rhinoceros beetle

≪ lady beetle

Summer Nature Camp

What's better than friends, fun, and bugs?

Join us for a summer you'll never forget!

1 We have exciting news to share! This year's summer camp will focus on insects. There are lots of fun new activities for you. For example, we will hold an insect hunt. Each camper will receive a list of insects that live nearby. They will then try to find as many of these insects as possible. Once they find one, they can take a picture of it. The camper with the most finds wins a prize!

2 All our campers will become insect experts. They will know the difference between a lady beetle and a rhinoceros beetle. But more importantly, they will also learn to love and respect nature.

3 There are only so many spaces, so sign up today!

Session 1: June 1st – July 1st

Session 2: July 2nd – August 1st

Session 3: August 2nd – September 1st

Price: NT$15,000 for one session

Sign up at www.naturecamp.com

Q UESTION

_____1. **What is this reading mostly about?**
   a. Insects.   **b.** A camp.   **c.** Lady beetles.   **d.** Summer.

_____2. **What is the main idea of the second paragraph?**
   a. Campers will learn about rhinoceros beetles.
   b. Campers will win a prize.
   c. Campers will learn a lot about nature.
   d. Campers will enjoy the activities.

_____3. **What would be the first day of camp in Session 2?**
   a. August 2nd.   **b.** September 1st.
   c. June 1st.   **d.** July 2nd.

_____4. **"Price: NT$15,000 for one session." Is this a fact or the writer's opinion?**
   a. Fact.   **b.** Opinion.

_____5. **Linda sent an email to her friend about the summer camp. Below is the email.**

Date: Monday, July 15, 2020
Subject: Save some money on summer camp

Hi Tony,

I just found a coupon for the summer camp. We can use it to save NT$2,000 each session. Just enter "INSECTSAVE" when you sign up. Maybe we can now go to two sessions now? That would be great.

Linda

How much will they pay for a session if they use the coupon?
a. NT$5,000   **b.** NT$13,000   **c.** NT$17,000   **d.** NT$10,000

» blooming Queen
of the Night

Night-Time Beauty

↑ seed

1   For show-and-tell this week I want to show everyone my favorite plant. I know what you're all thinking—it doesn't look like much. But once a year, this ugly-looking plant produces a beautiful white flower. There are many special things about this flower. It only opens at night. And it only opens for a few hours before it dies. It has a very short life, but it's a very special one. The flower is big—17 cm wide and 30 cm long. And the smell it gives off is wonderful—so strong and sweet. It fills the whole house.

2   This plant is originally from South America. There, it grows high up in the trees of the forests. But here, people grow them in their gardens. And they invite people over to watch them open once a year. Oh! I forgot to tell you its name. Because it's so beautiful, people call this flower the "Queen of the Night"!

QUESTION

_____1. **What is this talk about?**

    a. A famous queen.   **b.** South America.

    c. A special flower.   **d.** A beautiful garden.

_____2. **How big is the Queen of the Night?**

    a. Seventeen centimeters wide and three centimeters long.

    b. Thirty centimeters wide and seventeen centimeters long.

    c. Seven centimeters wide and thirty centimeters long.

    d. Seventeen centimeters wide and thirty centimeters long.

_____3. **Which of the following is NOT true about the Queen of the Night?**

    a. It only opens at night.   **b.** It has a bad smell.

    c. It only opens once a year.   **d.** It dies after a few hours.

_____4. **Which of the following might the speaker compare the flower to?**

    a. The full moon.   **b.** A red apple.

    c. A dog's tail.   **d.** The world's highest mountain.

_____5. **Below is a table from a book on South American plants.**

Alstroemeria aurea	*Cattleya labiata*
Grows in bushes of up to 1 m high. Produces small yellow and orange flowers. Flowers last for several weeks.	Grows up in the trees. Produces large purple flowers with a weak but sweet smell.

Epiphyllum oxypetalum	*Plumeria rubra*
Produces large white flowers with a strong, sweet smell. Flowers open only at night.	A popular garden plant. Produces small pink, white, and yellow flowers. Lives mostly in deserts.

Which of these is most likely the Queen of the Night?

    a. *Alstroemeria aurea*.   **b.** *Cattleya labiata*.

    c. *Epiphyllum oxypetalum*. **d.** *Plumeria rubra*.

🎧 45

45

How Can You Say I'm Brave

≫ brave

1

I'm not a soldier or a fighter

I'm not a mountain climber or a lion hunter

I don't fight **crocodiles**

or wrestle bears

or swim with sharks

at the bottom of the ocean

I don't jump out of planes

or put on a suit

and climb into a rocket

and fly up, up, up

into cold, dark space

How can you say I'm brave?

≫ hunter

≫ wrestle

2

How? Let me tell you:

Because **you get back up every time you fall**

Because you smile, even when you want to cry

Because you **take a step forward,**

even when you feel like lying down

Because you make choices, even when they're hard

Because you try, even though you might not **succeed**

Because you **face** things, even when they frighten you

Because you never, ever, ever give up

That's why I say you're brave

QUESTION

_____1. "I don't fight crocodiles / or wrestle bears." **What is a "crocodile"?**
   a. A kind of airplane.   **b.** A special soldier.
   c. A dangerous animal.   **d.** A foreign language.

_____2. **What does the writer mean by** "you get back up every time you fall"?
   a. You don't let mistakes stop you.
   b. You don't like to be wrong.
   c. You often make bad choices.
   d. You don't feel angry when people laugh at you.

_____3. "Because you take a step forward, / even when you feel like lying down." **What does the writer mean by** "take a step forward"?
   a. Take a break.   **b.** Keep on going.
   c. Fall over.   **d.** Make a mess.

_____4. "Because you try, even though you might not succeed." **What is the opposite of "succeed"?**
   a. Win.   **b.** Fight.   **c.** Sleep.   **d.** Fail.

_____5. "Because you face things, even when they frighten you." **Which of these phrases has the same meaning as "face" here?**
   a. Give away.   **b.** Look at.
   c. Deal with.   **d.** Make up.

The Moon's Mirror

1   Some call it the "Moon's Mirror" because of its **oval** shape and still, clear waters. Others call it the "Angel's Tear" because of its **deep** blue color. Chiaming Lake isn't the largest lake in Taiwan, but to many, it is the most beautiful.

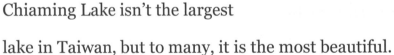

2   People used to think the lake formed 3,000 years ago when a **meteor** fell from space and hit the mountain. But in fact, it is even older than that—around 7,000 years old. And it really formed when a large river of ice cut out a piece of the mountain.

« space

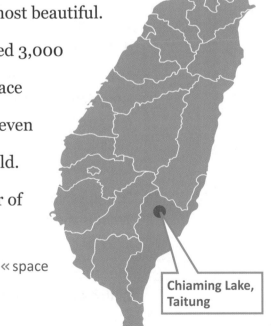

Chiaming Lake, Taitung

3 The lake is not easy to get to, however. At 3,310 m high, it is the second highest lake in Taiwan. Reaching it takes many hours of difficult hiking through the mountains near Taitung. But don't let that **put you off**. Many people make the long and difficult **journey** each year. And they all say it's worth it!

» hiking

QUESTION

_____1. **The writer says Chiaming Lake has an "oval shape." What kind of shape is an "oval"?**
    a. Having three sides.   **b.** Like a banana.
    c. Like a kite.   **d.** Long and round.

_____2. **The writer says Chiaming Lake has a "deep blue color." Which of these is the opposite of "deep" in this phrase?**
    a. Heavy.   **b.** Strong.   **c.** Light.   **d.** Dark.

_____3. **The writer says the lake formed "when a meteor fell from space and hit the mountain." What is a "meteor"?**
    a. A large rock.   **b.** A small ball.
    c. A flying animal.   **d.** A kind of airplane.

_____4. **What does the phrase "put you off" in the final paragraph mean?**
    a. Make you excited to do something.
    b. Make you not want to do something.
    c. Make you think something is easy.
    d. Make you pay lots of money for something.

_____5. **"Many people make the long and difficult journey each year." What is another word for "journey"?**
    a. Trip.   **b.** Train.   **c.** Road.   **d.** Map.

47

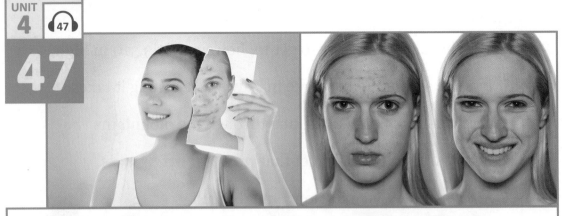

Winning the Fight Against Acne

» face wash

1   Is your skin **acting up**? Maybe you have blackheads, whiteheads, or other types of pimples. If so, you might have a skin problem called acne. There is good news though: you are not the only one. Acne is one of the most common skin problems out there. In the United States, some 40–50 million people have it. **Fortunately**, there are some things you can do to clear up your acne:

✓ Get outside and walk around. Exercise will help with acne and other health problems.

✓ Drink around 6-8 cups of water every day.

✓ Eat foods like beans, fruits, and vegetables.

 Give up the makeup.

Too much makeup can **damage** your skin.

 Avoid cleaning your skin too much in a day. Washing your face too many times can make your acne **worse**.

 Don't touch your face. Touching the pimples will just make them worse.

Get a bit of sun. Spend about 10–20 minutes outside every day.

QUESTION

_____1. "Is your skin acting up?" **What does "acting up" mean in this sentence?**
- **a.** Feeling strange.
- **b.** Doing something bad.
- **c.** Costing a lot of money.
- **d.** Making you feel good.

_____2. "Touching the pimples will just make them worse." **What is a word with the opposite meaning of "worse"?**
- **a.** Better.
- **b.** Simpler.
- **c.** Stronger.
- **d.** Later.

_____3. "Too much makeup can damage your skin." **What is a word with the same meaning as "damage"?**
- **a.** See.
- **b.** Feel.
- **c.** Hurt.
- **d.** Hit.

_____4. "Avoid showering more than once a day." **What does the word "avoid" mean in this sentence?**
- **a.** To not do something.
- **b.** To love doing something.
- **c.** To do something more often.
- **d.** To wash something.

_____5. "Fortunately, there are some things you can do to clear up your acne." **What is a word with the same meaning as "fortunately"?**
- **a.** Lately.
- **b.** Badly.
- **c.** Easily.
- **d.** Luckily.

» loving yourself
the way you are

Just Be Yourself

Sue: He really went too far this time!

Mark: What's wrong?

Sue: I'm still **worked up** about earlier

today. One second I'm arguing with

5   Robert about cars. The next second he calls me a tomboy!

What a jerk.

Mark: Tomboy? What does that word even mean?

Sue: It's what people call a girl who acts like a boy.

Mark: Oh. That sounds like people calling me girly for singing

10   popular songs all the time.

Sue: Exactly! These people seem to think that girls can't like cars, and boys can't like singing.

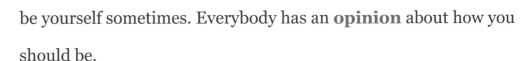

15 **Mark:** You know what they say: haters are going to hate. Just **ignore** them.

Sue: I know. But it can be hard to just be yourself sometimes. Everybody has an **opinion** about how you should be.

Mark: Don't worry about them. Worry about your **true** friends, like me.

20 **Sue:** Ha! So does that mean you'll talk about cars with me?

Mark: Not in a million years! Cars are **boring**.

QUESTION

_____1. **What does "worked up" mean in the sentence "I'm still worked up about earlier today"?**
   a. Happy.   **b.** Angry.   **c.** Tired.   **d.** Scared.

_____2. **In the sentence "Cars are boring," what is the word with the opposite meaning of "boring"?**
   a. Exciting.   **b.** New.   **c.** Loud.   **d.** Sad.

_____3. **What does "ignore" mean in the sentence "Just ignore them"?**
   a. To not notice something.   **b.** To try to fix something.
   c. To change something about yourself.
   d. To say sorry for something.

_____4. **"Everybody has an opinion about how you should be." What is a word with the same meaning as "opinion"?**
   a. Bag.   **b.** Gift.   **c.** Health. **d.** Idea.

_____5. **"Worry about your true friends, like me." What is a word with the same meaning as "true"?**
   a. New.   **b.** Polite.   **c.** Real.   **d.** Quiet.

49 Helping at Home

1   Do you help with washing the dishes after dinner? How about taking out the trash or cleaning the house? Many kids hate doing chores. But in fact, doing chores teaches you many important life skills.

≫ doing laundry

2   When you grow up, you'll need to know how to do laundry, cook, and keep your own house clean. Doing chores when you are young helps you become independent when you're older.

3   Chores also help you learn how to manage your time well. When you are a grown up, you'll have a job, friends, maybe even a family of your own. Having chores as well as schoolwork helps you learn how to manage a busy life.

⌃ taking out the trash/garbage   ⌃ vacuuming the floor   ⌃ washing the dishes

4   When I was younger, my mom gave my brothers and me lots of chores to do. She even wrote them all in a schedule. That way, we all knew what we had to do each day. Take a look at my old chores schedule:

	Lily	David	Phil
Monday	wash the dishes	walk the dog	take out the trash
Tuesday	walk the dog	take out the trash	help prepare dinner
Wednesday	take out the trash	help prepare dinner	clean your room
Thursday	help prepare dinner	clean your room	wash the dishes
Friday	clean your room	wash the dishes	walk the dog
Saturday	clean the house	clean the house	clean the house
Sunday	do laundry	do laundry	do laundry

QUESTION

_____1. **What was Lily's chore on Wednesdays?**
   a. Do laundry.   b. Walk the dog.
   c. Wash the dishes.   d. Take out the trash.

_____2. **On what day did David have to clean his room?**
   a. Monday.   b. Thursday.
   c. Friday.   d. Wednesday.

_____3. **How many times a week did Phil have to walk the dog?**
   a. Once.   b. Twice.   c. Three times.   d. Four times.

_____4. **Which of the following is TRUE?**
   a. Only Lily and David did laundry on Sunday.
   b. Lily washed the dishes on Tuesday.
   c. Everyone cleaned the house on Saturday.
   d. Phil helped prepare dinner on Wednesday.

_____5. **Which of the following was NOT one of the children's chores?**
   a. Help prepare dinner.   b. Wash the car.
   c. Take out the trash.   d. Clean their rooms.

Sharing Your Life With Others

1   Do you use social media? The answer is probably yes! Almost everyone uses some kind of social media these days. People love to add friends, post messages, and upload their photos and videos.

2   One of the first social-media sites was Classmates. It began in 1994. People used it to find old school friends. But not many people use the site anymore. And many of the other early social media sites are no longer around.

3   More recent social media sites include Instagram, Snapchat, and TikTok. The last two are very popular with young people. They let you share fun videos of yourself with the world.

4   On the next page is a timeline of some of today's most popular social media sites and apps. A timeline tells you when things happened. Timelines start with the earliest event and end with the most recent.

A Timeline of Today's Most Popular Social Media Sites

2002

Linked .
A social media-site for business people. People use it to meet new business partners and find new jobs.

2004

facebook.
A social-media site originally only for university students. Now for everyone over the age of 13, it has more than one billion users.

2005

You Tube
The first popular video-sharing website. People post videos of everything from their funny pets to their travel experiences.

2006

twitter
A social-media site for people to post very short messages to their "followers."

2010

Instagram
A site mainly for posting photos—especially of food! Many famous people now use it to sell things like makeup and beauty products.

2011

snapchat
This app lets you send videos and pictures to your friends. But they will disappear quickly. It is very popular with teenagers.

2016

TikTok
A Chinese video-sharing app. People mostly use it to create short videos of themselves singing and dancing.

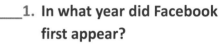

Q UESTION

_____ 1. In what year did Facebook first appear?
a. 2002.
b. 2004.
c. 2006.
d. 2010.

_____ 2. Which of these social media sites/apps came first?
a. Twitter.
b. Instagram.
c. YouTube.
d. TikTok.

_____ 3. What it TRUE about Instagram?
a. It is mainly for posting photos.
b. Photos on Instagram disappear quickly.
c. It was originally for university students.
d. It first appeared in China.

_____ 4. Which social media site/app appeared in 2011?
a. Twitter.
b. Instagram.
c. LinkedIn.
d. Snapchat.

_____ 5. Which of these social media sites/apps appeared after YouTube but before Instagram?
a. Facebook.
b. Twitter.
c. TikTok.
d. LinkedIn.

Translation

Unit 1 | 閱讀技巧

1-1 明辨主題／歸納要旨

01 奇特的新語言 P. 20

網路是個奇特的世界，彷彿是擁有自己的語言的獨立國家。以下列出幾個常見的網路用語和釋義，幫助大家學習網路語言：

網紅：在社群媒體擁有許多粉絲的人。（例句：「最近似乎人人都想當IG網紅。」）

主題標籤：意指接在某措辭或短語後的「#」字號。
大家常會以主題標籤來標明發文的主題。（例句：「我剛買了一些金屬吸管。#拯救地球」）

爆紅：如果有影片、照片或故事「go viral」，這表示該內容在網路上被迅速瘋傳。
（例句：「強尼的舞蹈影片爆紅，已經超過百萬點閱率了！」）

酸民：在網路上發表無禮或苛薄言語的人。（例句：「別再對我的照片留下難聽字眼了，你這個酸民！」）

網民：泛指經常上網的人。（例句：「台灣網民超愛觀賞美食類的YouTube影片。」）

02 戴口罩的文化差異 P. 22

羅伯：哈啾！

康詩坦絲：唉呀，你好像感冒了。要不要我給你一片口罩？

羅伯：謝謝妳，但為何要戴啊？我已經生病啦。

康詩坦絲：那正好是戴口罩的重要時機啊！你不想傳染給其他人吧？

羅伯：等等，妳的意思是，這裡所有戴口罩的人都已經生病了？

康詩坦絲：沒錯，這是在地文化的一部分。生病卻不在公共場所戴口罩的話，會被覺得沒有禮貌。

羅伯：現在想起來，這還挺有道理的。西方國家幾乎沒有人戴口罩，而且如果你與人交談但不露臉，對方還會覺得你沒有禮貌。

康詩坦絲：那你現在想戴口罩了嗎？

羅伯：當然要戴！我可不想無禮。畢竟，住在一個不同的國家，最大的好處就是學習新文化。

03 男人能跳草裙舞嗎？ P. 24

你聽說過夏威夷草裙舞嗎？大家常以為，草裙舞的舞者多是穿著草裙的女性，但其實男性也可以跳喔！

在過去，學好草裙舞對夏威夷男人來說相當重要。如果你是個優秀的草裙舞舞者，就代表你有能力成為優秀的戰士。所有男人都想成為驍勇善戰的鬥士，所以他們需要接受許多訓練，好變得敏捷強壯。

即使到了現代，夏威夷男人仍會跳草裙舞。但他們不靠上健身房來鍛鍊身體，而是依循人們過去的方法，在海裡游泳，並背負重石沿著沙灘跑步，他們甚至會爬上椰子樹頂。

現今的男性草裙舞舞者不想打鬥，他們只想謹記祖父與曾祖父的古法。草裙舞不只強化他們的體能，還有他們的心智。

04 平安度過新冠肺炎 P. 26

冠狀病毒的種類繁多，有些只會造成不大嚴重的普通感冒，有些卻很危險。新冠肺炎病毒入侵人體後會繁衍數量，使我們生病。新冠肺炎容易在人與人之間傳染，還可能讓我們病重致死。

如果帶源者對著我們近距離打噴嚏或咳嗽，我們就有可能感染到新冠肺炎。我們還可能因為碰到患者接觸過的物體而染病。如果我們手上帶有病毒，又用手去觸摸臉部，一樣有可能罹病。為了防止大家感染病毒，醫師建議大家應該勤洗手，並彼此保持安全距離。

我們現在一定要記得保護自己，才能在下次有危險病毒時做好準備。

05 來自朋友的舉手之勞 P. 28

週二真諦

克萊爾·史密斯 撰

即使是芝麻小事，也能讓人領悟出重要道理，是不是很奇妙呢？

我前幾天在網路上看了一部逗趣的影片，是關於巴西小藍鳥的。為了尋覓女友，鳥兒必須借助兩位朋友的幫忙。牠們每天苦練艱難的求偶舞，直到完美了，才肯在母鳥面前大展舞姿。如果母鳥舞藝夠精湛，就會讓帶頭的公鳥當牠的男友。

起先我被這些小鳥傻呼呼的舞姿逗得哈哈大笑，但我隨後想起，我的朋友總是幫助我克服困難。我才領悟到，有朋友在必要時刻及時援助，這是多麼棒的一件事。

因此，我這週二的真諦就是：要對你的朋友心存感激，因為他們能幫助你完成不可能的任務！

1-2 找出支持性細節／理解因果關係

06 珍重再見，詹姆斯老師！ P. 30

親愛的詹姆斯老師：

很難過聽到您下週要離職的消息。我一定會非常想念您的。您在這學期教會了我許多重要的事情，包括增進我的寫作能力、運用新詞彙，還有正確的發音。但更重要的是，您教會我相信自己。

去年的我，上英文課時都會很害羞。我怕犯錯，所以不喜歡舉手。但您教導我，勇於嘗試才是重要的，就算犯錯了也沒關係，因為我能從錯誤中學習，也才能更加進步。

因為您的緣故，我現在變得更有自信。希望您回到美國後也不會忘記我們全班，我們會一直思念您的。

敬祝安康
2A 班的莉莉

07 挑戰判斷力 P. 32

珊卓：嘿，路易！你好嗎？

路易：喔，嗨，珊卓。

珊卓：你怎麼悶悶不樂的？發生什麼事嗎？

路易：我弟弟住院了。

珊卓：傑克嗎？為什麼？

路易：他因為「三人跳挑戰」而受傷。

珊卓：那是什麼？

路易：那是一種新的惡作劇方式，很愚蠢又危險，是從美國傳過來的。

珊卓：是什麼樣的惡作劇呢？

路易：會有兩個人讓第三個人站在中間，騙他說他們要拍三個人一起跳起來的影片。當中間的人跳起來的時候，旁邊兩個人就一起踢中間人的腳，讓他背部著地跌倒。

珊卓：聽起來真危險。那傑克上當了？

路易：對啊。他兩個「朋友」整他的。他現在背部受重傷。其他被整的人，還有頭部撞地導致腦部受損的，甚至有兩個小孩還因此不治！

珊卓：太可怕了！希望傑克趕快好起來。

路易：他會的，謝謝妳。只希望他下次小心一點。

08 聊聊動物 P. 34

你的弟弟是超級學人精（copycat）嗎？朋友說故事的時候，你常覺得事有蹊蹺（smell a rat）嗎？外面是否下著滂沱大雨（raining cats and dogs）呢？英文有許多動物相關的用語，但到底是什麼意思？又是源自何處呢？

學人精：小貓會複製母貓的動作來學習成貓的習性。如果你模仿某人的穿著或言行舉止，你就像小貓一樣，是個學人精！

感覺事有蹊蹺：在過去，老鼠隨處可見，還會散播疾病，但狗可以聞到老鼠的蹤跡並加以驅趕。你覺得有人在散播謊言或作弊嗎？那麼你就像是聞到了髒老鼠的狗一樣呢！

下著滂沱大雨：很久以前，瀑布（waterfall）也可叫做「catadupe」。

時代更迭下，這個字演變為「cats and dogs」，所以說「it's raining cats and dogs」就是指雨下得跟瀑布一樣（也就是滂沱大雨的意思！）。

---

09 該是破除成規的時候了！ P. 36 ....

藍色適合男孩，粉紅色適合女孩——這不是定律嗎？也許不是喔。

這個觀念是從 1950 年代才開始普遍的，在此之前，大家對於男孩和女孩最適合什麼顏色並沒有共識。那時有些育嬰雜誌甚至認為，粉紅色適合男孩（因為較亮眼），而藍色適合女孩（因為較漂亮）。事實上，大約 150 年前，所有孩童不分男女都穿白色洋裝。

那麼我們現在為何會有這樣的觀念呢？大公司為了能更容易賣東西給我們，造就了現代的顏色規則。如果你是女孩，當你看到粉紅色的物品，會不由自主認為「啊！這很適合我」，你就很有可能將它買回家。

當然囉，不論是男孩喜歡粉紅色，還是女孩喜歡藍色，這都完全沒有錯。當說到顏色，破除成規並無妨！

---

10 做出正確的選擇 P. 38 ....

潔絲：發生什麼事啦，老弟？

麥特：我朋友約我今晚跟他們去逛夜市。但我真的得待在家讀書準備我的考試。

潔絲：那你打算怎麼辦呢？

麥特：我不知道。我所有的朋友都要去。他們說我應該把考試拋諸腦後，跟他們出去玩。

潔絲：原來如此。要對朋友說不，是滿困難的。

麥特：對啊。我擔心如果待在家讀書，他們就不想跟我做朋友了。

潔絲：這個考試很重要嗎？

麥特：很重要，我真的需要得到一個好成績。

潔絲：我的建議是，別因為替自己著想而感到擔心，即使朋友不認同你也沒有關係。

麥特：但如果他們不再跟我做朋友呢？

潔絲：那表示他們本來就不是好的朋友。

麥特：我想妳是對的。謝啦，潔絲。

11 午後交通路況報導 P. 40

這裡是交通路況新聞，我是蕾西·喬曼。駕駛可以做好心理準備，今天下午在格林街附近會交通壅塞。今早 11 點半有部公車撞上路樹，造成車輛水洩不通，目前看來該段路況慘不忍睹。無人受重傷，但公車仍擋住了整個街道，如果您必須行經該區域，建議改經傑克森路。所幸警方表示，交通問題應可於下午 5 點前解決。

中央市場附近也是車水馬龍，由於場外舉辦美食嘉年華會，封閉了多條道路，恐怕全日均無法通過該區。最好的辦法是將車子停放在伯德街，再從此處步行或搭乘免費公車至嘉年華會。公車會停靠中央市場附近，今日車班時間為中午 12 點至晚上 10 點。接下來是氣象報告……。

12 開派對囉 P. 42

時間：2021 年 4 月 24 日星期五 4 點~
　　　2021 年 4 月 25 日星期六 11 點
地點：我家，溜冰場，滿月披薩餐廳
來自：比利·史密斯

大家好！

我會在禮拜五舉辦盛大的十三歲生日派對，大家下課後可跟我一起回家。我們可以把書包放在家，然後去溜冰。就算你們沒有溜冰鞋也不用擔心，我有溜冰鞋可以出借。

溜完冰後，我們會去吃披薩。滿月餐廳的有最棒的披薩！請先告訴我你們喜歡的披薩種類，好讓我先打電話去餐廳預訂。如果不喜歡吃披薩，餐廳還有其他選擇。在這之後大家可以一起到我家過夜，我打算在花園露營。我會準備好帳篷，但請大家自備睡袋。一定會很好玩的！

到時候見囉！

比利

13 別盲從 P. 44

大家好，我叫湯姆。我今天演講的主題是「別當盲從者」。去年我和朋友正在玩指尖陀螺，我們站在教室裡，正玩得不亦樂乎時，突然看到蘇西放在桌上的糖果。四下無人之下，我朋友叫我拿蘇西的糖果來吃。我知道那是不好的行為，但還是照朋友說的做，把糖果給吃了。

蘇西發現糖果不見後，嚎啕大哭起來。我感覺很糟，我聽從朋友指使而沒有自己思考。我隨後去書包拿出一些自己的糖果，把糖果給蘇西，並向她道歉，承認是我拿走她的糖果，她說沒關係，還覺得我的糖果比她的好吃。現在，我永遠會記得不該盲從，並且一定要三思而後行。謝謝大家的聆聽。

14 噓！新年別大聲嚷嚷 P. 46

當提到「新年快樂」，你也許會聯想到煙火、派對和歡聲，但在印尼峇里島可不是這樣過。在這裡，人們是用祥和寧靜的方式度過每年元旦。

這一天叫做「寧靜日／安寧日」（印尼文為「Nyepi」），在這 24 小時內，沒有人會離開屋內、大聲喧嘩、使用電力或生火，許多人還會全日禁食。這麼做是為了在新的一年開始前，好好淨化身心靈。

每個人均需慎重看待寧靜日，遊客也不例外。只有特種警察能上街，確保無人破壞秩序！

寧靜日可能聽起來嚴肅，但如果能熬過這一天，你將有意想不到的收穫。由於所有照明在寧靜日期間都是熄滅的，所以當晚夜空可清楚看見滿天星斗！對我來說，這樣的美景遠勝過煙火！

15 栩栩如生的皮影戲 P. 48

有些人用文字說故事，有些人用圖片說故事。但你知道，你也可以用影子說故事嗎？

皮影戲是一種獨特的說故事方式，源自數千年前（譯註：兩千多年）的中國。操偶師會坐在白紙幕後，幕後則有一盞照明燈。當操偶師操作紙製的人物或動物角色，人偶的影子就會出現在白幕上。優秀的操偶師能讓這些影子展現奔跑、跳躍、飛撲甚至打鬥等動作！皮影戲看起來總是十分刺激！

皮影戲在不同國家就有所不同：中國的皮影戲多以皇帝、皇后和英雄人物為主，但希臘的皮影戲則大多刻劃市井小民，非常、非常的逗趣。

可惜的是，時至今日，操偶師已所剩無幾，所以在此文化永遠失傳之前，你應該至少去看一場皮影戲。

1-4 綜合技巧練習

16 不能再有人生病了！ P. 50

格林老師：麥斯今天去哪裡了？

詹姆斯：他生病了，格林老師。他病得很重。

格林老師：不會吧！我們班每個禮拜都有人生病呢。麗莎，妳是不是上週才生病？

麗莎：對呀，詹姆斯和萊恩則是上上週生病。

格林老師：好，不能再這樣了，下週我們一定要做點改變。

詹姆斯：什麼樣的改變呢？

格林老師：我常看到學生摀嘴咳嗽。有誰可以告訴我，為什麼這樣做不恰當？

麗莎：因為細菌會沾在手上，摸到的東西也會因而沾染細菌。

格林老師：沒錯。所以我們大家咳嗽的時候，應改以手肘擋住，這樣就不會將細菌傳播至整間教室。

全班同學：贊成！

麗莎：喔，格林老師！我們還可以在進教室前，先用香皂洗手。

格林老師：好主意，麗莎。大家都同意嗎？

全班同學：同意！

格林老師：很好。希望從現在開始，班上生病人數會減少。

17 **斷捨離** P. 52

今年的暑期學生特賣會即將在下週六舉辦囉。你房間需要電子爐嗎?還是你想幫班上購入二手書?現在正是入手必需品的好時機。更棒的是,你買了還能省錢!

暑期學生特賣會已有超過 15 年的歷史。這活動是由一小群國際交換學生發起,當時他們想在回國前賣掉用不到的物品,而如今,特賣會已演變為學校的大型活動。

任何人都能在特賣會販售自己的物品。無論是包包或二手漫畫書,什麼都能賣,還會有美食飲品的特賣區。

走過路過,千萬別錯過!

時間:早上 9 點至下午 3 點半
地點:學生主樓前方
注意:如果需要設置販售攤桌,請在星期六之前,傳送電子郵件至林老師的信箱:
mikelin4464@hotmail.com。

18 **地表最強的網** P. 54

你可能怕蜘蛛,但你知道蜘蛛其實媲美小小工程師嗎?蜘蛛網十分強韌。有多強韌呢?某些研究顯示,若蜘蛛網的數量足夠,它的強韌度可比金屬高出五倍。想想看蜘蛛體型有多小;如果蜘蛛和人類一樣大,牠的網說不定能攔住一架飛機。

有些人試圖讓蜘蛛網再更加強韌。特倫托大學的學生正在研究蜘蛛絲,他們想改造蜘蛛,好產出更強韌的蜘蛛絲,進而有更堅不可摧的蜘蛛網。這項研究成果也許能應用於現實生活。想想看,以蜘蛛絲製衣的話,衣服不僅舒適還會堅固耐用。也許他們很快能研發出警察專用的特殊服飾,讓子彈也無法穿透,這樣一來,警察就會像超級英雄一樣刀槍不入了!

19 **誇張的購物行徑** P. 56

災難來臨時,大家都會萌生相同的想法。大家會想:如果商店都關門怎麼辦?如果我再也買不到食物怎麼辦?如果藥物兩週內就會缺貨該怎麼辦?因此,許多人決定開始大肆購物,甚至購買根本用不到的物品。這就是所謂的「囤貨」,也可以說是「恐慌搶購」。

但恐慌搶購行為會造成嚴重問題。店家的存貨無法讓每個人都買這麼多。這代表僅有一部分的人有辦法囤到貨,其他人則沒辦法,因為等他們到店裡時早就沒東西可買了。在這種情況下,問題已不再是災難造成,而是恐慌搶購行為本身。

你或許不會再歷經另一場災難,但假使未來有此情況,只買必要物品就好,這樣其他人才能也得到他們需要的部分。

20 野蠻男孩   P. 58

當你和一群同學被遺留在荒島上,會發生什麼事呢?你們會齊心協力設法生存嗎?還是會走到互相殘殺的下場?上述問題正出自於威廉·高汀於 1954 年出版的著作《蒼蠅王》。

故事大致在說,有架飛機墜毀在太平洋裡的荒島上,僅有一群年輕男孩倖存。剛開始的日子很愉快,但歡樂氣氛沒多久就消失殆盡。傳說中的可怕怪獸開始讓男孩們心生恐懼而抓狂,他們很快從一群好孩子,轉變為充滿獸性的野孩子。事實上,此著作最令人震懾的,不是怪獸或野蠻男孩,而是他們的小型社會以如此快的速度分崩離析。

如果你問我,我會認為每位年輕人都應閱讀此書,因為這本書中傳遞許多人人適用的重要道理。

Unit 2 ｜ 字彙學習

認識同義字與反義字／從上下文推測字義

21 久坐為何傷身?   P. 62

多數人能坐就不站,畢竟坐著實在舒服多了!然而新研究顯示,久坐是會傷身的。

這項研究調查了列車駕駛和鐵路局員工。兩組人員的飲食條件相同,但列車駕駛因為整日坐著而超重,鐵路局員工則因時常四處走動而體態正常。

變胖只是其中一項問題。久坐會對心臟有害。大家應該在白天活動,來保有健康的心臟。久坐還會對骨頭有害,如果不多走動,骨骼也會變得脆弱。最後,久坐會傷背,不出多久的時間,你看起來就會像英文字母 C(譯註:指駝背)!

醫師有些建議要給我們,他們說,內勤的上班族應該每 30 分鐘就起身一下,且不應整晚坐在沙發上,最好是做點運動。

22 一起加入戰鬥吧!   P. 64

《夢幻之戰》四月份競賽

最刺激的線上格鬥遊戲非《夢幻之戰》莫屬!大家要組成一隊奇幻角色參賽,運用魔法和絕招擊敗你的敵人。我們每個月會舉辦一次競賽,以選出最棒的《夢幻之戰》團隊。

你是《夢幻之戰》隊友之一嗎?你的表現能脫穎而出嗎?至下方報名,就能獲得贏取高額獎金的機會!

每場比賽至多能有 32 個團隊參加,請從速報名以免向隅。

日期與時間:　4 月 9 日星期六早上 9 點

23 我腦海裡的聲音 P. 66

我漂亮，但沒有你漂亮
我聰明，但沒有你聰明
我能跑得快，但沒有你快
我雖會唱歌，但沒有你的歌聲甜美

我希望能擁有你的所有天賦：
你的歌喉、你的頭腦、你的飛毛腿和你的長相
這些想法在我腦海裡揮之不去，讓我好生妒忌
為何所有我會的事，你都做得比我好

我的腦海裡出現這樣的聲音，一遍又一遍：
我希望你變醜、變笨、變遲鈍

我希望你唱的每首歌，聽起來都像鬼叫
這樣大家的眼神，終於會落在我身上

但我心裡浮現另一個溫柔的聲音：
如果我執迷不悟，永遠無法感到快樂
我必須接納事實；你是你，我是我
我不會讓自己以嫉妒心態度日

24 引起全球的注意 P. 68

格蕾塔‧桑伯格和一般青少年不一樣。年僅 15 歲的她，從 2018 年開始每週五翹課，為拯救地球而奔走發聲。乘網路之便，她的訴求得以蔓延開來。不久後，世界各地有超過兩萬名學生追隨她的腳步，開始翹課。

2019 年，她休學一年，希望專心做個領導者。該年九月，她前往美國參加探討氣候變遷的大型會議。因為她深信航空業有害環境，她拒絕搭乘飛機，而以帆船飄洋過海。她向全球各國領袖表達自己的憤怒，她認為他們未盡力拯救地球。此番演說撼動了許多人。

如今全世界都聽到了格蕾塔的聲音，她可說是年輕人喚醒全球注意力的最佳典範。

25 三項全能　P. 70

你擅長游泳嗎？那騎自行車與跑步呢？要贏得三項全能賽，你必須擅長這三項運動。三項全能賽堪稱世上最困難的運動之一。你要先游泳 1.5 公里，接下來是 40 公里的自行車程，最後則是 10 公里的長跑。最快完成全部賽程的選手即獲得勝利。

第一場三項全能賽是於 1920 年代在法國舉辦，但這項競賽一直到近年才變得熱門。光是美國，每年就有將近 50 萬人參加三項全能賽。

三項全能賽有許多不同種類，例如迷你三項全能和冬季三項全能。但最知名也最艱難的，就是鐵人三項。鐵人三項的賽程比一般三項全能賽多兩倍，只有頂尖的體能好手有辦法完成。你是好手之一嗎？

26 牙齒好痛！　P. 72

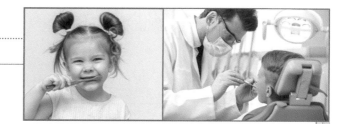

日期：3 月 23 日星期五

親愛的日記：

今天早上我的牙齒突然好痛。我痛到受不了，沒辦法吃東西，午餐的時候只喝得下溫水。

放學後，媽媽說我們要去看牙醫。我本來不想去，因為我怕牙醫。但又實在太痛了！所以我最後只好答應。牙醫檢查了我的牙齒，用東西幫我止痛，然後就開始處理牙齒。幸好醫師的技術高明，很快就結束了。

我離開之前，牙醫問我是不是很愛吃糖果或喝汽水。我告訴他，我確實吃很多。他說如果想要擁有健康的牙齒，就該停止這樣的行為。他也告訴我，每餐飯後都要刷牙。

日記啊，我保證從現在開始，一定會讓我的牙齒保持超級乾淨！

27 過猶不及，適度就好　P. 74

加點鹽巴，就能讓食物變得美味。但你知道攝取過多鹽分對大腦有害嗎？

紐約有科學家數週餐餐餵食老鼠高鹽分飲食，八週後，老鼠開始出現怪異行為。牠們健忘、不會築巢，還無法通過簡單的迷宮，而這些事情老鼠應該要能輕鬆駕馭的。如果套用到人類身上，就像我們變得不會穿衣、找不到教室或無法執行其他簡易行為。

那麼攝取多少鹽分才會導致異狀呢？幸好，答案是相當大量──大概是正常量的五倍到六倍。當然，現代生活裡隨處可見鹽分的蹤影，我們攝取的鹽分常超乎想像，不過別擔心，只要盡量保持健康飲食習慣，你吃進的鹽分其實傷害不大。

警告！
本區有小偷出沒！

昨天傍晚有人在本社區偷走一輛腳踏車。腳踏車的主人是住伍德街 21 號的居民詹姆斯・懷特先生，車子原本停放在他的花園裡。有鄰居目擊一名男子於晚上 7 點牽著懷特先生的腳踏車走在街上，該男子高挑，有一頭棕色長髮和長鬍子，身穿黑色外套，頭戴深藍色棒球帽。如果您看見此人，請立刻通報管區員警。

此外，請勿將貴重物品留在室外。腳踏車請停放於室內，並請記得將房車與所有門窗隨時上鎖。我們會盡力保護鄰里的人身與財產安全，也請大家配合保持警覺，協力逮捕小偷！

謝謝大家
管區員警

沉重的石塊能在沒有人力的幫助下自行移動嗎？答案是可以！這現象看似魔術般不可思議，其實不然，且僅出現於旱湖的湖床。

旱湖湖床指的是一塊乾燥平坦的地域。下雨的時候雨水會滲入湖床，入夜後天氣轉冷，表層的水面就會結成一片薄冰，浮在水的上方。到了早上，太陽升起，薄冰開始裂開，此時就會推動湖床上的石塊。這些石塊一分鐘可以移動五公尺遠！這相當於時速 0.3 公里。

多年來沒有人知道石塊如何移動，直到 2014 年，有人仔細研究這些石塊，他們在加州的死亡谷國家公園進行研究，以衛星導航系統，針對此類石塊長時間拍攝追蹤影片。

想到「家庭」，你腦海中浮現的畫面是什麼？是否有媽媽、爸爸和孩子？許多人對家庭的概念就是如此，但現今社會也存在很多單親家庭。

有些人認為單親家庭是破碎的。造成這類家庭的孩子常因此感到難過，但單親家庭真的有比雙親家庭差勁嗎？

請捫心自問——對家庭而言，什麼才是真正重要的？孩子是否感覺被愛？是否豐衣足食？是否健康且有安全感？如果上述答案皆為是，那麼單親與否真的重要嗎？當然不重要！

所以如果你來自單親家庭，千萬別覺得羞愧。重點不在於你有幾個家長，而是你擁有什麼樣的家長。如果你擁有超棒的媽媽或爸爸，請別怕去讚揚你的家庭！

Unit 3 學習策略

3-1 影像圖表

31 人體所需的養分 P. 84

你的身體需要若干養分才能良好運作,保持活動力需要熱量(我們以卡路里來計算熱量)。人體也需要蛋白質,蛋白質能幫助你成長,並有助於人體受傷時自我修護。人體可以用脂肪的形式儲存熱量,卻無法儲存蛋白質,因此每天攝取足量的蛋白質相當重要。

每個人每天一公斤體重需攝取 0.8 公克的蛋白質,假如你的體重是 65 公斤,表示你需要攝取 52 公克的蛋白質(0.8 x 65)。有些食物富含蛋白質,有些食物則較少。下頁的表格顯示當食物 150 卡路里時含多少公克的蛋白質。

表格能以縱欄與橫列的方式整理資訊。如果要查找每種食物含有的蛋白質量,請先從左欄開始瀏覽,再看至蛋白質那欄。

每150卡路里的蛋白質公克量	
食物	蛋白質
豬肉	23公克
壽司	12公克
牛肉	23公克
起司	16公克
牛奶	10公克

每150卡路里的蛋白質公克量	
食物	蛋白質
蛋白	24公克
番茄	1公克
蝦	11公克
甜甜圈	4公克
燕麥	4公克

32 家裡沒網路?沒問題! P. 86

我們現在幾乎能用網路做任何事情。我們上網看新聞,上網找用餐地點,上網和朋友閒聊等,擁有網路儼然成為一種人權。不過,有越來越多人不裝設家用網路,而是以手機上網。

結果,大家開始習慣「網路不離身」,使得人們越來越依賴他們的手機。我們都知道這樣有害健康,但現今仍有許多人已無法離開手機,即使只是幾分鐘的時間。

上頁折線圖顯示出美國成人擁有手機、卻沒有家用網路的百分比。折線圖會以「點」標示數據,再連接各點而形成折線,如此便於觀察長期以來的數據變化。

33 新家養新寵物 P. 88

我家沒有養寵物。我們住在都市裡的小公寓，爸媽說沒有足夠空間可以養。下個月我們就要搬到郊區較為寬敞的新家。剛開始我很生氣，但爸媽說，到時候就可以養寵物了！他們還說我可以選要養哪一種動物。我真的好開心，但我發現要養狗還是養貓實在很難選。

我畫了文氏圖來釐清思緒。文氏圖是以兩個圓圖所構成。在我的圖表內，一個圓圖裡是關於養貓的利弊，另一個圓圖裡則是養狗的利弊。兩圓中間會重疊，這區域我用來列出養狗和養貓的共同特點。現在我能清楚了解養這兩種寵物的異同處！

養狗		養貓
• 會聽話	• 必須餵食	• 可能會忽略你
• 可能會長到很大隻	• 可能會破壞家具	• 隨心所欲
• 總是很開心見到你	• 可養在室外或室內	• 不會去花園挖土
• 需要很多關注	• 可以撫摸	• 會清理自己
• 能教牠雜耍才藝	• 會到處掉毛	• 睡覺時數長
• 必須每天溜狗		• 會有可愛逗趣的行為
• 很愛主人		• 可以獨處好幾天
• 很吵		• 會自己在貓砂盆大小號
• 需要到室外大小號		• 不用帶去散步

34 當務之急的改變 P. 90

我們都喜歡在大熱天裡來杯冰涼的飲料。過去我們會用塑膠吸管來喝飲料，但時代變遷，現今許多國家已禁用塑膠吸管；如果你想用吸管喝果汁或奶茶，現在你必須用金屬或紙製吸管才行。

為何各國做出這樣的改變？因為塑膠吸管不會隨著時間而分解消失，卻會進入河流與海洋，傷害那兒的動物。塑膠還會瓦解成微粒，汙染水源與土壤。

可是我們真的有丟掉那麼多吸管嗎？真的有！請看下頁的長條圖，圖中顯示九個歐洲國家人民於2018年丟棄的吸管數量。長條圖以不同大小的長條形狀來代表數據，以便比較不同數據。

2018 年塑膠吸管的使用量（單位：十億）

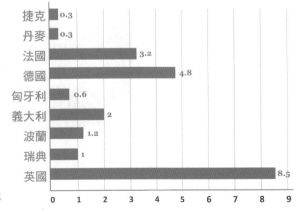

35 要不要看場電影？ P. 92

你最喜歡什麼類型的電影？你喜歡充滿打鬥槍戰的動作片嗎？還是笑料百出的喜劇片？那描寫困苦生活等寫實題材的劇情片如何？或許你喜歡的是充滿浪漫情節的愛情片，又或許你特愛以飛碟和時空穿越為主題的科幻片？

每個人都有自己喜歡的電影類型，但有些電影比較受男生歡迎，另有些較受女生歡迎。這就是為什麼，當你一群朋友中有男有女時，對於要看的電影很難取得共識！

我們在學校問了 100 名男孩與 100 名女孩，請他們說出電影喜好。結果顯示在下頁的兩張圓餅圖中。圓餅圖是以圓餅中的區塊來代表數據，區塊越大，表示數據越大。如此一來，就能輕易觀察出所佔比例最大或最小的數據。

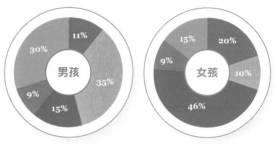

■ 喜劇片 ■ 動作片 ■ 愛情片 ■ 劇情片 ■ 科幻片

3-2 參考資料

36 大聲說出口！ P. 94

許多人害怕公開演講，光是想到這件事，他們就會緊張不已。但我們多數人的一生中，一定會有必須演講的時刻。

許多演講者犯的最大錯誤之一就是死背講稿。他們花好幾個小時記住講稿裡的每一個字，但其實這是最不可取的方法。較好的做法是只記住你的重點，這樣你才能更自然地發表演說，甚至可視情況迅速調整演講內容。

如果需要更多公開演講的建議，何不買本相關著作？一本好書可傳授各種實用訣竅和小撇步。下頁是《提升公開演講的能力》的目錄。目錄可顯示每一個章節的名稱／主題以及對應的頁碼。

目錄

37 可愛臉孔，危險殺手！ P. 96

河馬是大型的非洲哺乳類動物，牠們棲息於河邊，有著小巧的耳朵與偌大渾圓的灰色身軀，長得十分逗趣。然而事實上，河馬可說是世上最危險的動物之一。河馬性格易怒、牙齒巨大，還能跑得飛快，非洲每年死於河馬攻擊的有將近五百人。

有些人說河馬會流血汗！聽起來很可怕吧？假如是真的，那當然很可怕。河馬的汗水雖然是紅色的，但那並不是血，其實是一種特殊油脂，能保護河馬的皮膚不被非洲的艷陽曬傷。

我第一次看到「hippo」（河馬）這個字是在一本非洲相關書籍裡。因為不懂這個單字的意思，我當時去查了字典，並在「H」開頭的區塊找到這個字。現在看看那頁裡的其他單字，這些字都是以「hi」開頭的。

38 台灣的原住民 P. 98

台灣住了超過 2300 萬人，而大約 2% 出頭（將近 56 萬人）是台灣原住民。台灣原住民於數千年前來台，居住地曾遍布全台，但在 1600 年代，中國人和歐洲人紛紛踏上台灣島，攻擊原住民並奪取土地。如今，台灣原住民大多居住於台灣東岸和中央山脈。

台灣原住民共有 16 族，各族均有自己的習俗、節慶和語言。人數最龐大的是阿美族，約有 20 萬人左右。大家可從地圖看到，阿美族分布於台灣東岸的中段。此地圖亦顯示其他族的資訊，只要觀察一下地圖，就能得知台灣原住民的分布範圍。

39 絕佳旅遊好去處 P. 100

每年都有越來越多的外國遊客來台灣觀光，他們喜歡購買台灣大城市的零嘴，到墾丁附近的海邊衝浪，與攻克台灣最高峰。而且最重要的是，他們都玩得不亦樂乎！

觀光客要遊覽台灣很方便。以台北而言，隨時可搭乘捷運趴趴走！如果想遠離塵囂，只要搭乘短程遊覽車或火車，即可抵達日月潭等優美景點。

在台灣的遊客經常人手一本導覽手冊。手冊背後會有索引表，列出全書所有重點和查找用的頁碼。索引表會以字母 A 到 Z 的順序列出資訊。右頁是一本台灣導覽手冊的部分索引內容。

索引

---

40 美味的新料理 P. 102 ....

我今天去我朋友拉雅家念書。拉雅的媽媽問我要不要留下來吃晚餐,她媽媽是印尼人,而我真的很想吃吃看印尼料理,所以說:「好,麻煩了!」我們吃了印尼炒飯,雖然和台灣炒飯相似,但充滿更多風味,上面還放一顆煎蛋!印尼炒飯真好吃。我向拉雅媽媽請教食譜,下面是她寫給我的內容:

印尼炒飯

份量:4人份
食材

- 雞肉(50克)
- 蝦醬(2小匙)
- 甜醬油(3大匙)
- 蛋4顆
- 蒜頭(2瓣)
- 番茄2顆
- 紅辣椒1 條
- 小黃瓜1條
- 小洋蔥1顆
- 萊姆1顆
- 白飯(750克)

料理方式

1. 切碎辣椒和大蒜,放入炒鍋爆香。
2. 切碎洋蔥,一樣放入炒鍋爆香。
3. 雞肉切小丁,放入炒鍋翻炒至泛白。
4. 加入白飯、甜醬油和蝦醬,一起翻炒
   2分鐘。
5. 切碎番茄、小黃瓜和萊姆。
6. 煎蛋。
7. 每份炒飯上面放一顆煎蛋,附上一點番茄、
   小黃瓜與萊姆配菜,即可上桌。

4-1 閱讀技巧複習

41 **走上對的路** P. 106

選擇未來的工作：一些重要忠告

1. **花時間想想自己喜歡做什麼**

   你很有可能得投入一天中的大量時間在工作上，所以如果你能樂在其中，那就再好不過了！花點時間，思考一下你喜歡做的事情與原因吧。

2. **了解不同的工作種類**

   職業五花八門，試著去了解一下吧！如此一來，你才更有可能找到適合自己的工作。

3. **記得走出自己的路**

   別擔心學校其他同學想從事什麼行業。每個人都不一樣，這是你的未來，不是他們的！

4. **勇於嘗試**

   如果你想當作家，先去寫寫看校刊吧。如果你想成為足球教練，就先去打聽能否擔任校隊助教。親身去體驗看看那份工作是否適合你吧。

---

42 **未來之錶** P. 108

電子玩意兒現在隨處都是，像手錶、手機和健康監控裝置等，都是智慧型產品。但要買的東西實在太多了，如果有一個電子產品能一應俱全，該有多好？

幸運的是，還真有其物！

我說的就是 FitPro——這是大家從今以後唯一需要的電子裝備。想要傳簡訊給朋友？它做得到。想要查看你的心律數據？這它也辦得到。事實上，FitPro 幾乎能做所有事情，包括：

 • 播放音樂　　 • 每日記步　　 • 拍照

 • 地圖定位顯示　　 • 打電話

FitPro不僅實用，還長得很好看！它有三種不同的顏色：紅色、藍色與黑色，並由一些錶界大廠協助設計。

還等什麼？今天訂購 **FitPro**，即可享有 **$150** 折扣！訂購網址：**www.fitpro.com**

43 難忘的夏天 P. 110

大自然夏令營

有什麼比好友、玩樂、昆蟲還讚呢？
加入我們的行列，度過難忘的夏天！

我們有令人興奮的消息要分享！今年夏令營的主題是「昆蟲」，我們為你準備了許多有趣的新活動！像是會舉辦昆蟲挖寶活動，每位學員會收到棲息附近的昆蟲名單，學員要盡可能找到這些昆蟲；找到一隻昆蟲就拍張照，而找到最多昆蟲的學員就能贏得獎項！

所有學員都能成為昆蟲專家。大家會學會分辨瓢蟲和獨角仙的差異，更重要的是，還能學會珍愛與尊重大自然。

名額有限，今天就報名吧！

第一梯次：6月1日—7月1日　　報名請至 www.naturecamp.com
第二梯次：7月2日—8月1日
第三梯次：8月2日—9月1日
費用：單一梯次為 15,000 台幣

44 深夜綻放的美麗 P. 112

在這禮拜的發表會上，我想向大家展示我最喜歡的植物。我知道你們在想什麼——這株植物看起來不像是我會喜歡的東西。但每年一次，這株不起眼的植物會開出絕美的白色花卉。這花還有許多特色：它只在夜晚綻放，而且盛開幾小時後就會凋零，生命短暫卻十分精彩；它的體型挺大，寬 17 公分，長則有 30 公分；它聞起來濃郁甜美，滿室馨香。

這植物原生於南美洲，依著森林裡的樹高長。但在這裡，人們把它種在花園裡，而且還會邀請別人過來，一起欣賞一年一度的花期。喔，我忘記告訴大家這種花卉的名稱了！由於它如此美麗，人們都叫它「夜之花后」（譯註：曇花）！

4-2 字彙學習複習

45 你怎麼能說我勇敢呢？ P. 114

我不是士兵或戰士
我不能攀爬高峰或捕獵獅子
我無法和鱷魚或熊搏鬥
也無法與鯊魚在海底共泳
我不會從飛機一躍而下跳傘
也不會穿上太空衣、
爬進太空梭
飛向寒冷黑暗的太空
所以，你怎麼能說我勇敢呢？

怎麼說？讓我來告訴你：
因為你每次跌倒後，都能再振作起來
因為你即使想哭泣，卻仍然微笑
因為你就算想躺平放棄，卻還是邁步向前
因為即使為難，你還是會做出選擇
因為即使不一定能成功，你還是嘗試去做
因為即使你有所畏懼，仍然面對而不逃避
因為你永不、從不、絕不放棄
所以我說，你很勇敢

143

46 月亮的明鏡 P. 116

有人以其橢圓的輪廓和靜止清澈的湖水，賦予它「月亮的明鏡」的稱號；有人因其深邃湛藍的顏色，送給它「天使的眼淚」的美名——這就是嘉明湖，雖然不是台灣面積最大的湖泊，卻是很多人心中最壯麗的景色。

從前人們以為，嘉明湖是三千年前，太空的流星墜落撞擊山脈所形成。事實上，嘉明湖的歷史更悠久，可追溯至七千年前左右，且嘉明湖其實是由大片冰河切割山脈而成。

然而，要抵達嘉明湖並非易事。嘉明湖位於海拔 3,310 公尺的高山，堪稱台灣第二高的湖泊。要到嘉明湖，需穿越台東附近的山脈，費盡數小時路途艱困的登山步道才行。不過別因此卻步了。每年還是有許多人克服漫長困難的征程，異口同聲不虛此行呢！

47 戰痘攻略 P. 118

你的皮膚出現狀況嗎？你或許有黑頭粉刺、白頭粉刺或其他類型的痘痘，而如果你有，那你可能患有稱為「青春痘」的皮膚病。但好消息是，你不孤單。春春痘是最為常見的皮膚問題，約四千萬至五千萬名的美國人有這困擾。幸好你可以採取以下對策來消滅青春痘：

- ✅ 出外走走。運動有助於改善青春痘和其他健康問題。
- ✅ 每天飲用 6 至 8 杯水。
- ✅ 多吃豆類、水果和蔬菜等食物。
- ❌ 別化妝。太多彩妝品有害皮膚。
- ❌ 避免每天過度清潔皮膚。洗臉太多次，反而會使青春痘惡化。
- ❌ 不要觸碰臉部。一直摸痘痘只會讓患處更惡化。
- ✅ 曬點太陽。每天走出戶外約 10 至 20 分鐘

48 做自己就好 P. 120

蘇：他這次真的太過分了！

馬克：怎麼了？

蘇：我還在氣剛剛的事。我才正和羅伯特爭論車子的事，他竟然接著叫我 tomboy（男人婆）！真是混蛋。

馬克：Tomboy？這個詞是什麼意思？

蘇：這個詞是人們用來稱行為舉止像男生的女生。

馬克：喔。聽起來就像大家說我女孩子氣，就因為我老是在唱流行歌曲。

蘇：就是啊！那些人好像總認為女生就不能喜歡車子，男生就不能喜歡唱歌。

馬克：你知道，俗話說「有的人就是什麼事都看不順眼」。別理他們就好。

蘇：我知道，但有時真的很難做自己。大家對於別人該怎麼做都很有意見。

馬克：別擔心他們的看法，只要在意像我這樣的真心好友就行啦。

蘇：哈！所以意思是，你會跟我聊車子嗎？

馬克：想都別想！車子太無聊啦。

4-3 影像圖表複習

49 幫忙家務 P. 122

你吃完晚餐會幫忙洗碗嗎？那會幫忙倒垃圾或打掃家裡嗎？許多小孩都討厭做家事，但其實做家事能教會你許多重要的生活技能。

長大以後，你需要學會洗衣服、烹飪與保持家裡整潔。趁早做家事，能幫助你長大之後變得獨立。

做家事還能讓你懂得好好規劃時間。成年之後的你，會有工作、朋友，甚至是自己的家庭，所以現在兼顧家事和課業，能讓你學會應對往後忙碌的生活。

我小的時候，媽媽會分配許多家事給我和兄弟做。她還會寫成一張行程表，讓我們清楚每個人每天該做的家事。大家可看一下我以前的家事行程表：

	莉莉	大衛	菲爾
週一	洗碗	遛狗	倒垃圾
週二	遛狗	倒垃圾	幫忙準備晚餐
週三	倒垃圾	幫忙準備晚餐	整理房間
週四	幫忙準備晚餐	整理房間	洗碗
週五	整理房間	洗碗	遛狗
週六	打掃家裡	打掃家裡	打掃家裡
週日	洗衣服	洗衣服	洗衣服

50 與他人分享生活 P. 124

你有使用社群媒體嗎？答案大概是有吧！現今幾乎人人都在用社群媒體，大家都喜歡互加好友、發表訊息與上傳照片和影片。

社群媒體網站的始祖之一是Classmates。Classmates創立於 1994 年，當時大家用這個網站來找以前的校友。然而現在沒什麼人會用它了，還有很多早期的社群媒體網站，現在也都紛紛關站了。

近年新興的社群媒體網站包括Instagram、Snapchat 和 Tiktok，其中又以後兩者深受年輕人的歡迎，因為用戶能把自己的有趣影片分享給全世界。

下頁的時間軸是以一些當今流行的社群媒體網站與應用程式為主題。時間軸告訴你各事件發生的時間，並且依照事件先後順序來排列。

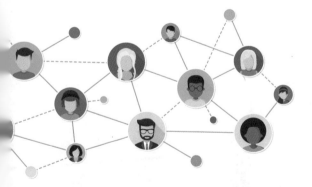

現今熱門社群媒體網站的時間軸

2002

LinkedIn
商務人士專用的社群媒體網站。大家用此網站認識新的商業夥伴與找工作。

2004

臉書
原先為大學生專用的社群媒體網站，現使用年齡門檻僅為13歲；為用戶超過十億人的網站。

2005

YouTube
堪稱熱門影片共享網站的先鋒。大家可上傳逗趣寵物、旅遊經驗等包羅萬象主題的影片。

2006

推特
專門讓人向粉絲發表極簡訊息的社群媒體網站。

2010

Instagram
以上傳照片為主的網站，尤其是美食照片居多！ 許多名人現在還會以IG來銷售美妝品。

2011

Snapchat
能讓人向朋友傳送影片和照片，但檔案很快就會失效。十分盛行於青少年族群。

2016

TikTok
來自中國的影片分享應用程式。用戶大多拍攝自己唱歌跳舞的影片。

Answer Key

Unit 1 閱讀技巧

1	1.b	2.a	3.c	4.d	5.b	11	1.d	2.a	3.c	4.b	5.a
2	1.b	2.a	3.c	4.a	5.c	12	1.b	2.b	3.b	4.b	5.d
3	1.b	2.d	3.d	4.a	5.c	13	1.c	2.a	3.c	4.b	5.c
4	1.a	2.c	3.c	4.a	5.c	14	1.d	2.c	3.a	4.d	5.a
5	1.d	2.a	3.b	4.c	5.c	15	1.d	2.a	3.b	4.a	5.c
6	1.a	2.d	3.a	4.c	5.b	16	1.b	2.c	3.d	4.a	5.c
7	1.c	2.b	3.a	4.d	5.c	17	1.b	2.b	3.a	4.d	5.b
8	1.d	2.a	3.b	4.c	5.c	18	1.b	2.a	3.d	4.c	5.b
9	1.c	2.b	3.a	4.d	5.b	19	1.a	2.c	3.a	4.d	5.a
10	1.c	2.b	3.c	4.a	5.c	20	1.c	2.b	3.b	4.a	5.d

Unit 2 字彙學習

21	1.d	2.b	3.d	4.a	5.b	26	1.a	2.b	3.c	4.a	5.d
22	1.c	2.b	3.d	4.a	5.b	27	1.c	2.a	3.d	4.b	5.d
23	1.b	2.a	3.c	4.d	5.a	28	1.a	2.d	3.c	4.a	5.b
24	1.d	2.b	3.a	4.c	5.d	29	1.c	2.b	3.b	4.a	5.b
25	1.d	2.b	3.a	4.c	5.b	30	1.b	2.a	3.a	4.d	5.a

Unit 3 學習策略

31	1.c	2.b	3.c	4.d	5.a	36	1.c	2.d	3.a	4.a	5.c
32	1.a	2.c	3.b	4.d	5.c	37	1.c	2.c	3.b	4.d	5.b
33	1.a	2.d	3.b	4.d	5.b	38	1.d	2.b	3.c	4.a	5.d
34	1.a	2.c	3.b	4.d	5.b	39	1.d	2.a	3.a	4.c	5.a
35	1.c	2.d	3.a	4.d	5.c	40	1.b	2.c	3.d	4.a	5.c

Unit 4 綜合練習

41	1.a	2.c	3.b	4.b	5.d	46	1.d	2.c	3.a	4.b	5.a
42	1.d	2.a	3.b	4.d	5.a	47	1.b	2.a	3.c	4.a	5.d
43	1.b	2.c	3.d	4.a	5.b	48	1.b	2.a	3.a	4.d	5.c
44	1.c	2.d	3.b	4.a	5.c	49	1.d	2.b	3.a	4.c	5.b
45	1.c	2.a	3.b	4.d	5.c	50	1.b	2.c	3.a	4.d	5.b

讀出英語核心素養

核心素養

九大技巧打造閱讀力

作者	Owain Mckimm
協同作者	Zachary Fillingham (2, 17, 18, 19, 42, 43, 47, 48)
	Laura Phelps (3, 11, 21, 29)
	Rob Webb (4, 12, 13)
	Richard Luhrs (7)
譯者	劉嘉珮
審訂	Helen Yeh
企畫編輯	葉俞均
編輯	王采翎
主編	丁宥暄
圖片	Shutterstock
內頁設計	鄭秀芳／林書玉
封面設計	林書玉
發行人	黃朝萍
製程管理	洪巧玲
出版者	寂天文化事業股份有限公司
電話	02-2365-9739
傳真	02-2365-9835
網址	www.icosmos.com.tw
讀者服務	onlineservice@icosmos.com.tw
出版日期	2024 年 8 月 初版再刷（寂天雲隨身聽 APP 版）(0104)
郵撥帳號	1998620-0 寂天文化事業股份有限公司

國家圖書館出版品預行編目 (CIP) 資料

讀出英語核心素養 1：九大技巧打造閱讀力
（寂天雲隨身聽 APP 版)/ Owain Mckimm 等
作；劉嘉珮譯 . -- 初版 . -- [臺北市]：寂天文
化，2022.02-
　　冊；　公分
ISBN 978-626-300-107-7
（第 1 冊：平裝）

1. 英語 2. 讀本

805.18　　　　　　　　　　　111001881

訂書金額未滿 1000 元，請外加運費 100 元。

〔若有破損，請寄回更換，謝謝〕